WITCHBORNE

RACHEL GROSVENOR

First published 1st September 2025 by Fly on the Wall Press
Published in the UK by
Fly on the Wall Press
56 High Lea Rd
New Mills
Derbyshire
SK22 3DP

www.flyonthewallpress.co.uk
ISBN PBK: 9781915789426
EBook: 9781915789433
Copyright Rachel Grosvenor © 2025

The right of Rachel Grosvenor to be identified as the author of this work has been asserted in accordance with the Copyright, Designs and Patents Act 1988. Cover design and typesetting by Isabelle Kenyon.

All rights reserved. No part of this publication may be reproduced, stored in or introduced into a retrieval system, or transmitted in any form, or by any means (electronic, mechanical, photocopying, recording or otherwise) without prior written permissions of the publisher. Any person who does any unauthorised act in relation to this publication may be liable for criminal prosecution and civil claims for damages.

A CIP Catalogue record for this book is available from the British Library.

EU GPSR Authorised Representative
LOGOS EUROPE, 9 rue Nicolas Poussin, 17000, LA ROCHELLE, France
E-mail: Contact@logoseurope.eu

*To my nieces, Robyn, Auri, Uma, and my nephew, Noah.
May you never have to hide who you truly are
(wonderful, each of you).*

Content warning:
childbirth, child loss.

If we refuse to render the tithes to God, that he will take away
the nine parts when we least expect it
and we will also have increased our sin.

I Æthelstan

SANGUIN SPRING

Chapter One

Fire. In the distance, the church bells began to peal, the tones shifting and pulsing against Agnes' ears, signifying that a ceremony was about to begin.

Agnes pushed her hands into the furnace, watching the flames lap at her skin without heat. She would not go to church today. The embers were too tempting. For a blacksmith's daughter, hers was a noble and sensible gift from the Gods, and this charm was given to her on the day of her birth by the Grothi.

In her small town of Locklear, an ancient tradition persisted: every female child, born as the spring blossoms unfurled, received a mystical gift. The town's lore, rich with elaborate passages and lyrical sayings, spoke of this custom's deep roots and the vital role of nurturing their daughters. Though the old texts were verbose, their essence could be distilled to a single, powerful notion: these gifted women would not only bear the next generation, but also serve as its guiding light.

Agnes stretched her hand out further, watching the skin barely redden. Her gift was unique, she knew this much. No one else had it. In fact, the other gifts that had been bestowed were nowhere near as special. Her mother had realised early on that Agnes' gift was different, and in fear of her being outed as a witch, Gods forbid, she had pretended that it was something else. So, day by day, when asked, Agnes displayed her charm. She could bind water, she said, bring it from stream to house. Of course, she used a bucket for this, and as such, this charm couldn't be said to be much of a gift, but it served its purpose. It stopped the people of Locklear from thinking that she was special.

"Agnes!" Her mother's voice filtered through the iced air. Hastily, she pulled her hands from the flame and turned, offering up a smile.

"Morning, Mother."

"How many times have I told you to stay away from the furnace? What if somebody sees you?"

Agnes shrugged, glancing around at the steel on display at her father's forge, merely a lean-to attached to their wooden house. He had been working hard on an order from the kingdom, a hundred swords for the war effort.

"I should think they would believe I am a blacksmith's daughter, Mother."

"You know what it is I refer to."

Agnes did. Her gift was too special, too obvious. Only the Gods knew what they had given her, and her mother had said they must have been wrong to do so. Blasphemy. The Grothi was the voice of reason, the bridge between the Gods and the people, and yet it was said that even he didn't know what gifts he bestowed on the girls on those strange spring days. Agnes doubted this, she saw the way he stared at her occasionally. To suggest that the Gods had made a mistake was blasphemous enough, words not to be uttered among the townsfolk.

"Agnes." Her mother snapped her fingers, about to dig deeper into a lecture, when a cheery greeting rang out, and Saskia, the local celebrated beauty, came into view.

Agnes watched her mother's expression change entirely, a swooping look of faux delight changing her features. "Saskia! What a gift from the Gods to see you this fine morning. I hear that your mother has been hard at work preparing for the Spring Feast?"

Saskia glanced at Agnes, a look that hid a wealth of disdain from her mother, and wrinkled her nose. They were the same age, and in a town as small as Locklear, they had no choice but to see each other often. And yet, Saskia made her intentions quite clear. They were not friends, however much she might imagine Agnes should want to be. In reality, Agnes cared not a jot for Saskia, forced into her acquaintance by nothing but coincidence.

"She has ma'am, of course. It wouldn't be the Spring Feast without her cooking, would it?" The barb was a small but well-crafted one, an indication that Agnes' family had little to offer in comparison. This was, in some ways, true, but it didn't stop them from trying to contribute. They baked a pie, offered cider, but it was usually left to the side in favour of the more delectable offerings delivered by Saskia's family. Agnes glanced at her mother, feeling the sting, and saw a twitch in her cheek. She had noticed it, too.

"Ah, of course it wouldn't, child, and we look forward to her offering."

Saskia turned her attention to Agnes, who was still sitting before the furnace, her blackened apron in stark contrast to Saskia's clean one. "Agnes, dear, will you join me at the stream? Mother needs water for steaming the pastry. It's more than one bucket."

Having said not a single word and reluctant to part her lips, Agnes merely nodded. Had she not, she knew she would face a cross remark from her mother. She stood and picked up the old, dented bucket that her brother had made many years ago during his apprenticeship and glared at her mother. Had she been left alone to heat up the furnace, she could have ignored Saskia and pretended that she hadn't even seen her.

*

The stream was high that morning, rushing over stones. To Agnes, it seemed both clear and dark at the same time, as though full of secrets.

Agnes had wound up carrying both buckets. Quite how this had happened wasn't clear to her, but she watched as Saskia smoothed down her pristine apron and lightly sprang across the grass in her fine leather sandals, her straight, clean toes quite at odds with Agnes' muddied and crooked bare feet.

"Tell me, Agnes, do you have your eye on any boys yet?" Saskia asked, her voice not quite sincere. Agnes glanced over. The truth was that, no, she hadn't. She knew that Saskia often spent evenings at the tavern, but this was something her parents would never agree to. She had never so much as stepped foot in it before, the raucous laughter that came from within was enough to deter her.

"Not really," she responded quietly. She noticed that Saskia was watching her, her eyes bright with delight.

"Oh, well, I'll tell him not to bother then."

Agnes felt her cheeks flush. She didn't know what Saskia was referring to at all, but the word 'him', as though there really was a 'him', watching her from afar, was enough to cause her skin to tingle.

"What do you mean?" she ventured, unsure if she truly wanted to know.

Saskia paused, scratching a bare forearm absently, as though the secret she was about to bestow was of little interest. "Ah, it's nothing. Just that the tanner's son said something about you." The words came out as a sort of purr, gleeful and sour.

Agnes took a breath. The tanner's son? She wanted to know, but if she leapt to ask, Saskia would mock her. She had been mocked before and knew that the best thing to do was to act as if she cared not, so that nothing could touch deeper than breath on skin. Agnes rounded her shoulders, sniffed the air as though recalling a distant memory, and asked, "What did he say?"

Saskia turned, eyes wide, mouth wider, and bared her teeth in sheer delight. "He said he thinks you're pretty. He wants you to come to the tavern tonight, so come with me, and I'll introduce you."

The empty buckets clanged together as though answering Saskia, though it hadn't been a question. It had been phrased as a statement, a demand. Who was this girl to be making demands of her? Just because Saskia's mother had once worked in the royal palace kitchens years ago, the way the family carried themselves, you would think that they were royalty themselves. Agnes didn't even know if it was true. The towns beyond Locklear were nothing but secrets, the kingdom nothing but words and laws. The King and Queen didn't visit Locklear, but trusted the Grothi to lead the people. If Saskia's mother truly had worked in the kitchens of the royal palace, she had certainly come back a person of Locklear through and through, untouched by other cultures.

Agnes rolled her eyes with just as much rebellion as she could muster and leaned forward until she reached the stream. With care, she filled the buckets until they were three-quarters full, and handed one to Saskia, being genuinely careful not to drop any on her fresh, clean clothes. Saskia took the gift with a smirk and sighed wistfully as they began to walk back to the town.

"Your gift was fetching water. Do you know what mine was?" she asked, sing-song voice cloying in Agnes' ears.

"You weren't born in the spring, so you didn't get one from the Grothi."

Saskia's head snapped towards Agnes, and her eyes darkened. "Actually, I was born on the cusp of spring, and so the Grothi bestowed a gift on me anyway."

That wasn't true. Agnes knew it wasn't. She wouldn't have been surprised if Saskia's mother had paid the Grothi just for the action, pretending that her daughter had been gifted. Agnes kicked a stone and looked up at the sky, seeing the clouds flicker darkly, a promise of rain hanging over the fine day. Did the Gods know about Saskia's lie? Did they care? Agnes had seen other women lie in the town about gifts; she also knew what secrets did to families. They tore women from their brood, took them away, hung them in the woods.

"My gift was the gift of love." Saskia's voice filtered through Agnes' thoughts, and she glanced at her, listening. "I can match just about anyone in true love. That's why Showl left town last year. I introduced her to the farmer's son the next village over, and they fell in love. Now she's pregnant."

Agnes wrinkled her nose. Showl had not gone to live in the next town over. People didn't leave Locklear with such levity. She had been accused of witchcraft. Saskia's words were strange, and Agnes wondered what her mother had truly been telling her. She was childlike, even for her young age. Seventeen was old enough to know where Showl had really gone, wasn't it? Agnes had been told by her own mother under the cover of darkness.

"And you may be my greatest accomplishment if all goes to plan tonight, Agnes." In her enthusiasm, Saskia kicked her own bucket and caused a wave of water to fly over the edge onto the path. She didn't notice. "You do not have many altogether desirable qualities. Your brother, for one thing..." The sentence died in her mouth, and Agnes picked up her pace, trying to move past her. She didn't want to talk about her brother. She didn't want to be pregnant; she didn't want to be married to the tanner's son. She didn't even know who he was.

In the distance, she could make out the figure of her father, stoking the flames of the furnace. If she squinted, perhaps it could have been her brother, after all. But no, not now. His abandonment of the family had besmirched their name.

"And tonight, Agnes," Saskia called, and Agnes realised she was strides ahead now. She moved her head to the side to indicate that she was listening. "Tonight, try and wear something a little less…filthy."

Agnes bit her tongue hard, tasting blood, not responding. She was a blacksmith's daughter, practically a blacksmith herself. She was forged in the flame and dirt.

Chapter Two

Agnes felt the weight of the Gods' scrutiny. Life was laid out thus. Obey your parents, who sought both your safety and their future comfort. Heed the Grothi, whose lips dripped with holy wisdom from the Gods. And above all, a woman must watch, wait, and hold her tongue—for silence was her prescribed virtue.

Her mother's warnings about Agnes' gift echoed in her mind, a constant reminder of unseen dangers. There was a tale, oft-whispered, of a girl from her mother's youth who had wielded her blessing for dark purposes.

"How?" Agnes had once asked, leaning forward and trying to climb into the story, to learn it by heart. Her mother's response was always the same: a furtive glance skyward, as if the very act of remembering might draw unwanted attention from above.

"This is what you must know to survive," she'd say, her voice barely above a whisper, the weight of unspoken consequences hanging in the air between them. "She possessed a rare blessing, perhaps even rarer than your own."

"I know no one with my blessing, Mother."

"And so it ever shall be, Agnes, because your blessing is a secret and not a soul shall know. This girl, she was quiet, but she came alive around a few people. I was one of those, though for what reason I have never been able to fathom. When we walked together to the stream she would sing and talk, divulge her secrets and share gossip. You know, child, that I am not a gossip. One day, Agnes..."

There was a pause as her mother waited for a nod of the head. To be a gossip, Agnes knew, was not a good thing. It meant that you could not keep a secret to yourself, that you could not be trusted. Her mother looked about her, though there was no one but themselves sitting by the stove.

"This girl had seen a woman in town with a man who was not her husband. With the man, she was sharing her gift and more besides. As plain as your own hand appears when you move it in front of your face, this girl I knew followed them into the woods, watching. Caring not for decency or for where a woman should be, she illuminated the pair for the town to see. Agnes, her gift was the power of light. Just as with her personality, she could turn it on for whom she chose. But on this dusky evening, her emotions were fraught enough to get the better of her. In her righteous anger, she cast a light so brilliant it rivalled the sun." Agnes' eyes widened. "The entire town stirred, drawn to the otherworldly glow, like moths to flame. By the time they arrived, the couple stood exposed, clothed, but caught in their sin. And the girl...she couldn't extinguish her light. It burned and burned, fuelled by her fury and shame." The story ended abruptly. Agnes had cleared her throat, shook her head.

"What?"

"The Grothi bid that we go home. He put the light out." Her mother's face was still, matter-of-fact.

"So, how do you know of the circumstance? Of the man and the woman and—"

"Because she screamed it, child. Over and over, even as they dragged her away."

Silence enveloped them, broken only by the crackling of the hearth. The message was clear: a woman's gift, misused, could bring ruin not just to herself, but to all who shared her blood. To speak out was to invite disaster.

*

Locklear, a town of barely a thousand souls, pulsed with life as darkness fell. Though distant from the royal seat, the blessings of the King and Queen were bountiful throughout the Principality of Hargothrest. As night descended, the town's lifeblood—its taverns and drinking holes—began to stir, their cellars well-stocked and ready to fuel the local economy.

Agnes stood before the tavern's weathered door, her presence there a riddle even to herself. She hadn't wanted to come and had explained the situation to her mother through hesitant lips. To her astonishment, her mother's reaction had been nothing short of jubilant. She had clapped her hands and hollered out of the window for her father, who had solemnly nodded and touched his forehead, a sign that he was thanking the Gods.

"You're seventeen, Agnes. We cannot keep you forever. It is time that you went, that you found your own story."

So now she stood, wearing her mother's best apron (still stained a little, but nowhere near what else was on offer). Her mother had braided her dark hair, but not before tutting at the greys that had appeared at the front and plucking them out. She was wearing her brother's old shoes, boots, that had fit him long before his disappearance. She wriggled her toes beneath the hard leather and wished desperately that she were free of constraint.

There, a glimmer of light on the horizon of the town square, was Saskia. Her apron appeared cleaner than ever, and she, too, had braided her hair, dried flowers now settling in a crown atop her head. Agnes watched her come closer, saw the surprise in her eyes as she acknowledged her presence.

"Agnes! You came. And you look…well, quite presentable. You even brushed your hair. I am impressed. Have you been inside yet, seen if your betrothed awaits?"

Agnes said nothing but shook her head, the thought of stepping into the din behind her a horrifying claw in her side. She felt her hand being plucked from the air and found herself being driven within the wooden walls of noise. This was where the men were. This was where she should watch her footing.

The scent was the first thing to hit her. It was the yeasty smell of her mother baking bread, the smoke of the wood fire and pure sweat. The air pulsated with the taste of bodies. Agnes didn't have to look around to know that men filled the room. The atmosphere was thick with testosterone, something that Agnes avoided day to day. She allowed herself to be led by Saskia, whose confidence was impressive. She stalked through the tavern as though she were born to be there.

"Friends!" her voice trilled. Agnes looked up at the table ahead of them, several men, or perhaps more likely boys, around their age, sat drinking from flagons. They grinned at the arrival of Saskia. Agnes noticed a little nudging of elbows.

"This...is Agnes." She released her hand and pushed her forward with a gentle shove, a lamb to the slaughter. Agnes found herself nodding, trying a smile, as the boys looked her up and down. To feel their eyes upon her was terrible, like insects crawling across her skin. She shook slightly as if to dislodge them.

"Cold, Agnes?" one of the boys asked, and Agnes noticed that his eyes were not unkind. It was a genuine question. She knew that this could not be the tanner's son, he was far too clean.

"Yes, I am a little," she responded. A lie.

"Come then, take a seat, and Saskia will fetch you an ale. We don't bite." The boy smiled, and Agnes accepted his offer, pulling up a stool.

"This is Silo," Saskia interrupted, indicating a different boy. "He's the tanner's son."

Agnes glanced at Silo. He was wearing a blood-stained apron, his face grim from a hard day's work. She knew why you should always stay upstream from the tanner, knew that in the streams of Locklear his father and he washed their wares free from urine in the water. By the look of him, he hadn't washed himself in months. Out of politeness, Agnes nodded. Silo stared at her with tired eyes, a lazy gaze trickling across her skin.

"Agnes," he said, his voice low.

A barmaid wandered over with a tray of ale and silently placed the full cups down, collecting the empties. Agnes stared at the one in front of her. She had never tried ale, never tasted the yeasty brew, and felt out of her depth among these new people. She watched as Saskia pulled up a stool and took a deep drink of her own pint.

"So, Agnes was desperate to come and meet you all. I told her that some of you are taken..."

Blood rushed to fill Agnes' ears, and she felt her skin grow hot beneath the glares. She was not desperate to come and meet these boys, quite the opposite. Saskia was making it sound as though she herself had asked about them, as though she had begged to be introduced.

"Your pa's the blacksmith, right?" the kind boy asked. Agnes nodded. "He does fine work. I'm Finn, by the by."

Agnes glanced back to Silo, who was now staring at the wall with a hard look of boredom.

"Silo, won't you come and sit beside Agnes?" Saskia suddenly said, prodding Agnes in the ribs. She moved the table around until satisfied, and Agnes noticed that she was now sitting beside Finn, leaning in and whispering in his ear.

Sitting beside Silo increased the scent of urine, and Agnes shifted slightly away as he leaned in closer. "Saskia tells me your brother left and that you're unengaged."

There was no question to answer, but Agnes found herself giving a slight nod, as he wasn't incorrect. But she was young, and Saskia was unengaged too, though you wouldn't know it from the way she was fawning over Finn. Agnes cleared her throat, feeling some sort of trick in the air. Had Saskia brought Showl, the girl she claimed to have matchmaded, here to meet her 'betrothed'? Had she known that the girl would be dragged into the woods not long after to hang from a tree?

"Yep," Silo went on, as though answering something. "Your brother betrayed your family. Your poor father will have to work himself into the ground now, won't he? All those years training him as an apprentice. Still, I hear he's got a contract with the kingdom, so he isn't blacklisted. Where did your brother go?"

If Agnes had known, she still wouldn't have said, but she didn't know for sure. She had heard her father speaking in hushed tones at night time, seen the handbill that they had discovered beneath his bed, pulled it from the rubbish when her parents weren't looking. Gone to join the war. To fight for the resistance. The handbill had spouted what her father called 'nonsense'. It said that the kingdom was against the people, that the King and Queen were not ordained by the Gods, that the true warriors of the land were the workers, who should be gaining all the benefits of their hard work, without owing tithes. That's where they had suspected him of going, but the truth couldn't be known. Perhaps he was dead, her mother had said. Perhaps that was better, her father had added.

"We don't know," Agnes whispered, her voice barely audible over the tavern's din. A strange memory came to her then, the way that grief sprinkled memories at inopportune moments. She saw her mother silhouetted against the hearth, dripping fat onto hot coals. The rich aroma would rise, embracing the rafters, enveloping their home in a comforting shroud. Agnes knew what it was for. She was trying to tempt her brother back, as though the scent might reach him wherever he had travelled to.

Silo's unwavering gaze pulled her back to the present. "You'll have to start looking after the family soon."

Agnes bit the inside of her cheek and reached towards the flagon in front of her, bringing it to her lips. The taste was strange to her tongue, earthy and sour all at once. She took a gulp, swallowing.

Undeterred by her silence, Silo pressed on. "The old saying is the truest, 'The daughter of spring shall look after her flock, her gift her reward for caring.' You collect water, don't you? A tanner requires more water than most."

With a silent grimace, Agnes saw that Saskia was now looking over at her, her eyes wide and watching. She gave her a strange sort of nod, a look of encouragement, of fervour. She was telling her to make more of an effort, Agnes knew. She didn't want to. To sit beside this urine-soaked stranger was quite enough. Wasn't she destined for more than this, than being the wife of a tanner's son? Hadn't she been given a real gift, a gift that would allow her to shape metal in the fire, to become a better blacksmith than even her father?

"Yes, I collect water," Agnes said, finding her voice. Saskia gave a nod of approval, before looking back to Finn. "I need a lot of water in my profession too."

Silo paused, a smirk playing across his lips. "Profession?"

"Yes. A blacksmith," Agnes said clearly. Silo shook his head gently, eyes twinkling as though she had just told a clever joke.

"You have a sense of humour. I like that. Come, drink your ale, and I'll walk you home."

Agnes did want to go home, wanted nothing more. Without a word, she drank the rest of her flagon. It wasn't a joke that she had made, and she desired to say so, but to do this would be to embarrass her father. He had already lost one child, and for another to humiliate him would be too much.

*

The moon guided their path, for the most part. Agnes' home was just beyond the town's edge, and she knew the tanner's dwelling stood further still. If she were truly honest, she had not expected Silo to either exist or be interested in her. A nagging sense of mischief lurked at the edges of her consciousness, and as they walked side by side, she couldn't shake the feeling that some unseen plan was unfolding.

Silo had been fairly silent, occasionally murmuring about the dry weather. The pungent scent that clung to him—whether it was his clothes or, Agnes dared not dwell on it, his very skin—was somehow more bearable in the open air.

"I don't mind, you know, about your brother," he said, suddenly. Agnes felt her boots sink into the mud beneath her and said nothing. What did she care if he minded? Who was he to mind, anyway?

"Agnes," Silo said, pausing. They were now beyond the square, past the main houses, and into the sparser streets, where the wooden buildings were spread wider. Agnes stopped, turning to his sincere face with confusion. "I would like to visit you tomorrow lunchtime to meet your parents."

A strange request, Agnes thought. Still, it was his day, and if he wanted to spend it with an older couple, then he was free to.

"As you wish," Agnes responded, starting forward again. She saw Silo sag as though the bones had disappeared from his body.

"Good," he sighed, laughing slightly. It was the first time she had heard him laugh all night.

Chapter Three

It was at around four in the morning that Agnes had put two and two together. Somewhere between sleep and wake, she had realised that Silo didn't want to come and visit her parents for the joy of it. He wanted something else. She swallowed into the darkness, tasting the ale that she had sipped hours before. Saskia had said that he thought she was pretty, and he wanted to come and see her parents. Was he to ask for her hand in marriage? Her stomach began to beat beneath the covers as though it had its own heart. A dull *thud, thud, thud* lulled her back to a hesitant half-sleep.

When she finally got up at five, her mother was already by the stove, stoking the flame. Agnes was hoping to sneak out of the door and head to the forest without a word, collect the water, dip her feet in the frozen stream, forget Silo and his request. When she had turned seventeen earlier in the year, she had been excited about what it would bring. Perhaps her father would start teaching her the family trade, finally allow her to hold the metal into flame and create something spectacular. She knew she had it in her, that her gift was not for nothing. What joy could there be in being a tanner's wife? She was surely too young for all that. And then, she thought of the other women in the village, of the stories her mother had told her about her own life. Childbearing years. And her, a spring baby, the ones with the responsibility. As her foot touched the straw floor, her mother spun around, eyes dancing.

"Agnes! You're finally awake. I saw you stir but thought it best to let you rest. We were asleep by the time you came home and—oh child, look at your hair!" She reached forward and began unbraiding the previously neat plaits, tutting and huffing at the mess they had become. Then, with a sigh, she continued her thoughts. "Tell me of last night. You met the tanner's boy?"

Agnes nodded.

"Tell me, girl, what are you holding your secrets for?"

Agnes braced herself. "He will be coming here at lunch to meet you."

Her mother did the expected. She grasped her hands to Agnes' heart and looked to the sky, muttering something beneath her breath. It was a prayer to the Gods, without doubt, and Agnes watched as the shape of her mother began to change. Her once low shoulders rose as though a guilt-laden blanket had been pulled from them. Her eyebrows raised, the gentle lines in her forehead increasing.

"My prayers have been answered, Agnes. Our prayers. Your father and I have been worried sick. Your brother leaving could have been the end of us, if the kingdom ever found out...but thanks to the Gods, with the new contract, and now your marriage to a respectable family, we will find ourselves back in good graces."

Agnes nodded slowly, considering her next words. She longed to unleash a torrent of shouts, growls, and curses. To proclaim that at seventeen, the weight of her family's future shouldn't rest solely on her slender shoulders. But deep down, she knew the bitter truth. If the kingdom ever uncovered—or even suspected—the real reason behind her brother's disappearance, her parents would be cast out. The solution was before her, as unpalatable as it was logical. By joining a new family, she could ensure her own safety and still support her parents from afar. This might be her only chance. Rumours spread fast. Think not of the dead girls hanging from the trees. As she opened her mouth to speak, her mother held up her hand and stopped her.

"Before you say anything, you should know this. Love does not come into a marriage. No marriage is born from love. You learn it, day by day."

So nothing was to be said, then. The words hung in the air, leaving no room for argument. Agnes felt the last vestiges of resistance crumble within her. What words could she possibly offer to counter such an immutable truth?

*

Silence stretched across the table along with her mother's best cloth, a tattered canvas effort. Agnes watched her father slice the bread, his lips a thin line. He had said almost nothing all day, in great contrast to her mother, who was clucking and fussing and bustling around the small house, straightening and plucking and sweeping. Silo had not yet arrived.

"Are you feeling well, Father?" Agnes asked, wanting a specific answer. She wanted him to declare that this was all for nothing, that perhaps Agnes should stand beside him at the furnace and help with the sword commission, that her gift would enable her to be the best blacksmith he had ever known. Instead, he picked up a crumb and placed it in his mouth, giving a weak smile.

"I am, Agnes. It's a day I have both hoped for and been wary of. I thought that your brother would come first, but...it was not to be."

He hadn't mentioned her brother in months. The words hung between them for a moment, and Agnes tried not to think of how he had let them, let her, down. If he were here right now, she wouldn't be entertaining the idea of Silo at all.

"I miss him," she said, three words she had not yet said aloud.

Her father's head snapped up, and his open face closed. "Enough of that. Thank the Gods that we have been given an opportunity. The tanner is a good man; his son has a fair profession." He leaned in, lowering his voice. "If anyone ever catches wind of where your brother is, we will be finished. Look brighter, Agnes, look happier. This is about saving our family's skin and nothing else. Right the wrong that your brother did us."

Agnes nodded, flinching as she heard the noise of footsteps outside on the path. Her father was right. It was up to her to correct the wrongs. She felt a sudden hatred flicker through her heart towards her brother. The line between love and hate was thin; she walked that tightrope for her entire family.

"He's here!" Her mother came hurrying into the kitchen, unwrapping the apron from behind her back. She pulled Agnes from her chair, touching the top of her head and flattening down any flyaway hairs. Her father walked towards and opened the door with great purpose, as though lowering the drawbridge for a prisoner.

"You are welcome, son of the tannery."

Chapter Four

The meeting had gone swiftly, with barely a word needed from Agnes. She had watched with bemused interest. Silo was wearing a clean cheesecloth shirt, his blood-splattered apron nowhere to be seen. He had clearly washed in the stream, the previous stench of urine now but a whiff in the air. The idea that his family might be able to procure soap was a surprise to Agnes, and yet she noticed his chewing of cloves, as though he were aware of the scent of his breath. His hair had been combed, his face shaved, and he had presented Agnes' parents with a clay jug, according to tradition. The effort that the boy had gone to was somewhat impressive, or at least, Agnes felt herself somewhere between impressed and annoyed. Where had her opinions gone, she wondered. The clay jug was a strange talisman in the centre of the table.

With barely an introduction, discussions had begun. The day of the Spring Feast was set for the wedding. Silo wanted a dowry, albeit a small one, to reward his kindness. At this suggestion, Agnes wrinkled her nose and received a swift kick under the table from her mother. All sorts of dowry were given and exchanged during weddings, though Agnes knew little of it. What did her parents have to offer? They suggested a wooden chest carved by her great-grandfather, the same dowry that her mother had brought to her father all those years ago. Agnes knew the chest well, had traced the curves of the wood, the stars and moons that adorned the surface, with her fingers many times. It was a comfort that this would be going to her new home, she thought.

"And Agnes, Father and I hope you are not afraid of a little hard work," Silo turned and said at one point, as though he had just remembered she was there. It was the first thing he had said to her. "As you know, my stepmother left us from sickness a year ago."

He turned back to her parents, touching his head and looking to the roof. "In these trying times, we must thank the Gods for their small mercies."

Small mercies. Agnes had let her attention wander, staring into the fire at the stove. She imagined herself standing, pushing her hand into the flame, showing her true gift to her future husband and demonstrating the real power that she had, far greater than his own. As if able to read her thoughts, her mother had laid a hand on her arm, pulling her back to the conversation.

"Agnes has many great skills and is a wonderful housekeeper."

Reduced to that, again, as women had been before her.

*

"Hold still, child. You move too much!"

Agnes glared at her mother, who was not so delicately pushing pins into the greying dress at her sides.

"You are too thin. You don't eat enough. Look at this space! When I wore this, I was your age, and it fit me like a dream. And now, I have barely a week to make preparations, and you lay this at my door!"

"Mother, how in the Gods–"

"Ah, child, you must away with that sort of chatter if you are to succeed in your new home."

Agnes bit her tongue, suppressing the urge to slap her mother's hands away. The dress clung to her skin in all the wrong places and hung loose in others. How could she have known, even a few days ago, that she'd be trying to fill this space—both literally and figuratively?

"And I need to get a gift for Saskia and her family. That girl is a true child of spring, regardless of when she was born. Her gift is a gift indeed."

Agnes scoffed, a bitter taste filling her mouth. "She doesn't have a gift." As the words left her lips, a pin grazed her side with uncanny timing, drawing a bead of blood.

Her mother's eyes flashed dangerously. "Gift from the Grothi or not, it's a blessing compared to your...affliction." She lowered her voice, glancing nervously at the windows as if the very walls might be listening. "Count yourself lucky, my girl, that he doesn't know your real power. With you as our daughter and your brother as our son, it's a wonder we haven't all been taken into the woods."

Agnes watched the top of her mother's head as she worked, sewing and biting at thread. Perhaps she was right. Agnes' power was too extreme, too volatile to be of the Gods, and her brother had joined the side of evil, against the Gods and their ordained.

"Aren't you afraid that the Gods can hear you, Mother?" Agnes asked, genuine curiosity mixing with a hint of defiance.

Her mother's hands stilled for a moment. When she spoke, her voice was barely above a whisper. "They know all. And should they be listening right now, I am sure they will understand that I am contending with the tests they have sent me the best I can. By next week, spring will be here, and this will no longer be of import. Now, stop talking. Every time you do, the fabric pulls and..." She paused, eyes travelling over Agnes' form with a mixture of love and exasperation. "Perhaps it would be best if you speak as little as possible on the day of the wedding. The dress suits you far better that way."

Agnes closed her mouth.

Chapter Five

"She is a promise-breaker."

The words rang out as Agnes followed her mother through the market. Her mother turned and flashed her a small smile, barely visible, but one that Agnes recognised well enough. Her mother always hissed at gossips, rolled her eyes at voices that dared rise above the crowd's murmur. Yet Agnes had learned to read the truth in the minute details: the way her mother's ear would prick, the slight tilt of her head. Nothing was spoken aloud. Her mother harvested the gossipy phrases from the market and sewed them into the tapestry of her memory. In the quiet hours of the night, Agnes knew her mother would pull out these threads for inspection, savouring each morsel of information. Agnes recognised this behaviour because, much to her chagrin, she found herself doing the exact same thing.

The sweet smells of the cabbage biscuits idled in front of her. Would she be allowed one today? "There's only money for the usual," was the refrain she'd grown accustomed to hearing. But occasionally, her mother would linger near a stall of delectable baked goods, her eyes darting about as if searching for something— or someone. If that occasion happened to coincide with Saskia's mother walking by at the same moment, Agnes might find a warm biscuit pressed into her hand. Once, Agnes made the mistake of calling it pride. Her mother tutted loudly and admonished her, "It is pride to buy my child a snack at the market, is it?" Alas, sometimes pride came before the biscuit.

But today, Agnes could not see Saskia or her mother in the market. They must have been getting ready for the wedding.

"Agnes, come and help me select the ribbons." Her mother linked arms with her, directing her over to the fabric stall. With a bright smile, she explained that Agnes would be getting married on the day of the Spring Feast, and how excited they all were.

"To the tanner's boy, Silo. So if you have white—"

"Ah, sorry, ma'am," the merchant said, his breath visible before him. "We're clean out of the white."

Agnes' mother paused, giving Agnes a look of pure amazement before she turned back again. "How could that be? Have you not prepared for the Spring Feast?"

The merchant glowered. Agnes didn't blame him and, in turn, was surprised at her mother. She saw how stressed she must have been, for she would never usually take such a tone with someone. "I am prepared if you please, but they have been bought out. We have yellow; that'll have to do." His stubby fingers jabbed at the pale yellow ribbons, and Agnes privately thought that they were very pretty indeed, perhaps even prettier than white.

"Well, yes. It will. A shame, for my daughter does not have blonde hair." Her mother selected two yellow ribbons and swapped them for coin, plunging them into her basket in irritation. As they turned to leave, she leaned into Agnes and lowered her voice.

"Who on earth buys out all of the white ribbons for the wedding day of many?"

The answer didn't need to be said; they both already knew. It was Saskia's mother, white ribbons to be placed in Saskia's golden hair to match her gloriously clean scent.

*

Try as Agnes might to delay the Spring Feast, it came trundling along as expected. She saw its arrival in the blossom on the trees, the green of the grass, the dried mud that clung to wet across the paths. The land began to bloom around her, and every day, she felt a small part of that inner bud wither. He hadn't visited, the man who was supposed to become her husband, and no one but she seemed to mind. Agnes had spent her days trying to remain by the side of her father, offering to help with the crafting of the swords, demonstrating her power to herself when no one was looking, and bashing out her fury into misshapen bits of metal that were no longer needed.

The Spring Feast was tomorrow. It was coming, and there was nothing she could do about it. Agnes stoked the fire of the furnace, gently slipping a coal from it into her hand, just to watch the embers die.

"Come, Agnes, did you shape this so?" Her father's voice moved through her mind, and Agnes turned her attention from the fire. He was holding a piece of metal she had worked on yesterday, a sort of diamond shape with a sharp point at the head.

"Yes, Father."

"Why, I'm impressed. Look here," he ran his fingers across the smooth edge and smiled, "you've done a fine job. A perfect little dagger, this would make. Just needs the hilt sorting, that's all."

Agnes stood and moved closer, watching the metal shift across her father's skin. "Really? You think it's good?"

"I think it's a fine effort, girl, especially without direction. If it pleases you, I can make a simple hilt, and that'll be a nice wedding gift from me. On one proviso, of course."

Agnes grinned, knowing exactly what it was. "I won't tell Mother."

That night, as darkness fell, Agnes climbed into her bed, feeling the familiar dip of the straw beneath her. It hadn't been changed all year. Late spring was the time for harvesting the straw, for re-stuffing the mattresses, and her bed would never be her own again.

Her mother had hung the grey dress on the back of her door, changes in place. Beside it, she had placed a flower crown that had taken her all week. These were signs that her mother loved her, Agnes knew, but she couldn't help but see them as signs that she was keen to be rid of her, to push her out of the door, flowers in her hair.

She took a sharp breath inwards, a stale and strange sickness settling in her stomach. Tomorrow. A tear would fall if she would let it, but Agnes would have none of it. What would it solve? There was no solution to be had. With a groan, she rolled over and pushed her hands under the blanket that lay beneath her head. Her fingers touched something smooth, and Agnes stretched them out, grabbing an object. She sat up and, in the darkness, stared at the finished dagger. Her father had tied a small string around it, a bow on the hilt. The tears that Agnes had been managing to hold back burst forth, and in silence, she let herself cry. She cried for her brother, for his selfishness and mislaid beliefs. She cried for her mother, for her desperation and forced hand. She cried for her father, for his loss and crumbling business. And she cried for herself, for a future that wasn't certain, a bed with an unknown entity and a house that smelled like piss.

*

The cockerel rose before all but not before Agnes on her wedding day. She was awake to hear its call, and with heavy eyes, she pulled back her covers, washed, and began to dress. Her mother had done a good job, it was true, and the grey gown fell upon her body like it had been made for her. She carefully plaited her hair, not wanting to leave it up to her mother, who would pull and tease, and placed the flowers upon her head. Though there was a small mirror in the kitchen, Agnes did not need it. No mirror could display how she truly felt inside. There was nothing to gain from looking.

In the kitchen, her mother waited by the stove, silent and hovering. It was a scene that Agnes had witnessed so many times. It had never before seemed special, important, or worthy, but now, the back of her mother, her long neck and the nape that was bared daily, the stretch of the hair into the tight plait across her head, suddenly seemed like the most special thing in the land. Agnes silently moved to stand next to her, watching the pot boil on the hob, and felt her mother's cool hand rest on her arm. There were no words, for her touch said it all. They locked eyes for a moment, and her mother smiled gently.

"After today, it will be over. It's just one day." With that, Agnes watched her busy herself making the morning soup, as though it were any other day. Her words were meant for comfort, Agnes knew, but they were really to comfort herself. After today, it would be over for her mother. Her life would be much the same, albeit quieter. Agnes' life would change entirely.

Chapter Six

The Spring Feast happened every year. It was an event that was looked forward to across the land. Pigs were slaughtered, corn gathered, berries crushed and fermented. Every household donated something of worth to the table, whether it be their clay pots to eat from or a large, triumphant pie that could feed the entire village (as in the case of Saskia's mother). It was the day upon which the Grothi invited the expectant spring mothers to the blessing ceremony at the end of the season, and a day that many decided to marry on. Agnes had heard that in larger towns and in the main city, the Grothi would stand in front of dozens of couples, his words applying to all, marrying them in one fell swoop. In Locklear, where the population was smaller, the Grothi took his time to bless each. They were lucky in this, her mother had reminded her. A Grothi's attention was akin to the gaze of the Gods.

Agnes and her family stepped out of their home, each holding a donation. Agnes held a loaf of bread her mother had carefully decorated in seeds, patterns displaying the night sky stretching from crust to base. Her mother held a rich, salted butter that she had been working on throughout winter. Her father held a bread knife he had made for the occasion, which he secretly hoped to get back at the end.

They quietly joined the rest of the townsfolk as they strode towards the field of plenty to place their wares on the table of devotion. As they walked, Agnes noticed the ground beneath her was hard and dry, a sure sign that spring had blossomed. The mud of winter had passed.

"Agnes!"

Agnes started. The sing-song voice was nearby. Her mother hissed something at her that she couldn't quite hear, but she understood the general direction: be polite.

"Agnes, wait!" With a pause, she turned to face Saskia.

She was dressed in a pure white linen gown, golden hair flowing behind her in waves. Flowers adorned her wrist, her head. Her cheeks were flushed pink, as though she had been complimented, and she brought with her a wave of the scent of honey. In comparison, Agnes felt filthy, even though she had washed.

"Agnes, wait until you hear," Saskia laughed, waving at her mother. "I'll be joining you in the wedding ceremony! Finn came to visit my parents, and it's all been arranged."

Agnes nodded, pushing her lips into a smile. A strange thought filtered across her mind, and she felt the touch of the spring breeze. She wished that she were on her way to marry Finn and that Saskia was to marry the tanner's boy. Surely, she mused, Silo felt the same.

"Congratulations, Saskia," Agnes said.

"Oh, Saskia, what delightful news!" her mother crowed, pushing the butter into Agnes' arms and kissing Saskia on the cheek. "A handsome couple you are indeed, and to think that you did us the kindness of gifting Agnes with marriage at the same time. Where is your mother? I must tell her what a blessing you are…"

Agnes watched as they wandered away through the crowd, a crowd that was, Agnes knew, led by Saskia's family, amid gigantic and impressive offerings.

*

Once the table was set, the Grothi arrived. The townsfolk stood in silence as he perused the donations, the feast before him. Truly, it was a large one this year.

"My friends, what a gift you have given to your country folk and to the Gods. Look at this bounty! This gift! This vision!"

Agnes leaned forward and scratched her ankle, a bug having alighted on her skin. The Grothi said the same thing every year, his ancient mouth spouting lines from between the crevices. As she stood up straight, she felt an elbow push into her side. Saskia was next to her and nodded to the left, indicating that Agnes should look. She did so. There, beside the end of the table, were a small group of young men waiting for their wives. At the front was Finn, his hair softly curling in the breeze, his cheek clean and shaved. He caught eyes with the two and winked, causing Saskia to let out a strange sound, a sort of giggle-exhale. Beside him stood Silo. Silo looked, Agnes thought, much the way that she did. He was wearing a greying cheesecloth shirt and had bags beneath his eyes that suggested a bad night's sleep. He didn't wink, catch eyes, or smile. In fact, he seemed to be making an extreme effort to do the opposite, his eyes focused so hard on the Grothi that Agnes thought he might be the one Silo was planning to marry.

"There they stand, our husbands," Saskia whispered.

With a slight shake of her head, Agnes held a finger up to her lips, pretending that the Grothi's words were fascinating to her. His speech was slow and plain, as always, and once done, he stepped aside to introduce the wedding portion of the day. Everyone waited in bored silence. No one cared about that bit if they weren't involved in some way, because it was the only thing that stood in the way of themselves and the huge display of food.

The boys spread out in single file, and Agnes counted five of them. Their parents stood behind them, and then the Grothi turned, his rust-coloured tunic blowing in the breeze, and raised his palms to the Gods.

"These children of spring have given themselves to your mercy, to the Gods, to their other half. They do so so that you might bless them with another child of spring and continue the glory of Locklear."

Agnes had heard the words many times before, every year since she was a child. And yet, she felt that she had never really paid attention until now.

"There are no gifts greater than the gift of love, the gifts that I bestow cannot be compared to..." the Grothi continued his monotonous drone. What was he really talking about? Did he have any idea that nobody was paying attention? Did he care? Agnes reached down to feel the small bite that had formed on her ankle.

"If we shall accept these blessings, as we must, in the light of the sunshine that you do so send down..."

Agnes let out a quiet sigh and stared ahead, waiting for the girls to be called upon to step forward. She looked at the expressions of the boys. The only one who seemed in any way joyful was Finn, who appeared to be trying not to laugh. The sight of his mirth, his teeth biting the inside of his cheeks, causing a strange dimple, and the light in his eyes, all made Agnes smile. A life with him would truly be a joy.

"And so, it is now that I ask the girls to step forward into their new lives, to go ahead and take their betrothed by the hands, and in leading their partners to take a bite of the food we have before us, they become husband and wife."

The Grothi turned to the five girls and beckoned. Something strange shivered through Agnes' mind, a bizarre and completely inappropriate thought. What if? What if she strode towards Finn, took him by the hands, and led him to the food? Would he follow her, change her prospects and fortune? With a hesitant step, Agnes walked forward with the other girls. Saskia was bounding along beside her, honey filling the air. As they reached the boys, Agnes took a sharp breath inward and stepped in front of the golden girl in the white dress. Finn laughed aloud, his brow furrowing, confused at the events. Without hesitation, Agnes pushed her hands into his and tried to lead him forward. He stood still, his face dropping from an astonished smile to an embarrassed glare.

"Agnes!" Saskia was beside her in an instant, batting her arms and pulling her hands away from Finn's. "Agnes, get off him!"

WITCH

The crowd began to whisper, silent jeers forming from within the ranks. Agnes stared into Finn's eyes and shook her head. No, she wouldn't let go. If marrying would save her family, she would do so, but she would marry the man she wanted. And that man wasn't Silo. Suddenly, there was a voice at her side. It was her mother.

"Agnes," she said, "let the poor boy go." Finn was now glancing around him, shrugging and trying to laugh, his eyes full of confusion. Agnes pulled once more, but the boy was stuck still.

Next, the Grothi tried. "Child, on a day such as today, you are under a lot of pressure. But you have chosen the wrong boy. Do you understand, child? You must move along to the next one, for the Gods have ordained it so."

Agnes could feel Finn's heartbeat through his hands, her own palms now slick with sweat. She shook herself, suddenly thinking of her father. How must this look to him? The embarrassment. With a shudder, she released Finn and tried to laugh, to give a light shake of the head. The Grothi breathed out a sigh of relief, grasping her by the shoulders, and he physically moved her down one place in the line. He manhandled her sweating hands into Silo's, who took them with force, and the two were pushed towards the table, where they involuntarily took a bite of food. Silo's eyes were dead and hard, and the way he stared at Agnes went right through her. He was embarrassed. They all were. Everyone except for Agnes, who was still having to stop herself from heading backwards, from pushing her hands back into Finn's.

The Grothi leaned in as she chewed and whispered in her ear, "You are a lucky girl. If you do anything like that again, you will suffer for it."

With shock, Agnes turned and looked into the man's face. He was wearing an expression she had never seen before, an expression of pure hatred.

"I am..." she began but was hushed by Silo.

"Do not worry, for we will discuss it later," he said beneath his breath. The men shook hands. Agnes licked her lips, reaching absently for another piece of bread, pushing it into her mouth. She turned as she chewed, to see the other couples eating at the table, Finn and Saskia among them. Finn had regained his laughter, whispering joyful nothings into Saskia's ear, whose eyes were wide with surprise.

"Silo." Agnes turned back to the man she was meant to be with for the rest of her life. "I apologise. A type of madness took over me."

He glanced around them and then leaned in close. "There's a price for everything, Wife."

And so began their marriage.

Chapter Seven

After every Spring Feast for her entire life, Agnes' family had forgone dinner. Why would dinner be needed when the spread put on by the town was so fruitful, so plentiful, so rich? They would weave their way home after dancing in the grass, laughing and rubbing their swollen stomachs, looking forward to the warm days ahead. When her brother had left the year before, the Spring Feast had been a sombre affair for them, but they had still danced, still eaten, and still pushed themselves to let laughs slither, albeit from downturned mouths.

Never had Agnes left early. But now, as the people of Locklear began to dance, as the band pulled out their fiddles and flutes, she found herself leaving the field. Her mother walked beside her, her father nowhere to be seen. Up ahead, her new husband walked beside his own father, talking beneath their breaths. Her mother let out a small cough, then spoke.

"Agnes, your behaviour today..." the words flittered into the air, unfinished. Her mother had nothing to say. "No marriage should start this way," she sighed finally. Agnes said nothing. When they got to the gate, the two men paused. Agnes' mother took her by the shoulders, staring sadly into her eyes. She leaned forward and kissed her hard on the cheek, leaving her scent of motherhood behind, the smell of home. Then, she stepped towards the men, shook both of their hands, muttered a word of apology, and was gone, walking back to the party.

"Come," Silo said, and Agnes obeyed, following the two men to her new home.

BORNE

*

The tanner's house was smaller than her own, a stone bridge crossing the stream that ran through town just before it, with a waterwheel adjoining. This element made Agnes smile, for her fake gift of bringing the water would perhaps be easier here than she had first thought. Large wooden structures surrounded the house, covered in rope and drying animal skins. The scent of urine and salt filled the air, coated her lips, and as they stepped onto the stone bridge she took a short breath, wondering when she might get used to the scent.

As they neared the door, her father-in-law opened it with a shove and stepped aside, indicating that Agnes should enter. The smell was worse inside if it were possible. How long would it take to ferment in her clothing, her hair? Her hands were clammy with sweat, and she was nervous. What would be said to her now that her parents were no longer there to protect her for her earlier actions?

She found herself in the kitchen, much the same as her mother's. A long wooden table stood before the unlit fire, logs surrounding the wooden wall. Dirty pewter plates and tankards were scattered on the top, memories of dinners past clinging to their surfaces. Bread lay cut on the side, as though it wouldn't stale, as though rats wouldn't get at it. These men knew nothing of caring for the homestead, Agnes could see, and there was a part of her that was grateful for it. Her hands would be busy, her presence felt, even through the embarrassment she had caused.

"Sit," Silo commanded, his voice laced with undisguised displeasure. He yanked a long bench from beneath the laden table, the wood scraping against the floor. Agnes lowered herself onto the seat, her grey dress suddenly feeling like a mockery of the occasion. Silo sat before her, barely looking at her face. Her new father-in-law began stacking logs up in the hearth, and Agnes realised that she hadn't yet seen what he really looked like.

"A tanner's day starts early. You will be expected to wake before us, to have the breakfast ready. After our visit to the butcher, we'll return expecting you to collect the discarded flesh and fat we remove from the hide to utilise in the kitchen. We rarely need to buy meat, Agnes, and we expect you to do a good job using every piece of gristle. Sometimes, we will be back for lunch. You will have supper ready by dusk. The water levels need to be kept topped up. This entire house must be kept in order, and this..." Silo indicated the current situation of the kitchen, "will not do."

Agnes nodded and opened her mouth to speak but was met with a raised hand. "I am going to take a moment outside. There are hides that need dealing with. A tanner doesn't get a day off just because it is the Spring Feast, Agnes. When I come back, I expect this place to be clean." With that, Silo stood and stalked out of the door, his hand grasping a bloody apron on the way. Her body was shaking, her skin tingling with ire. It was not unusual to be spoken to in such a manner by a man in the street, but a man in her own home? She drew in a shaky breath, memories of her father's patient ear and her brother's considerate demeanour rising unbidden. This man—her husband—was a stark contrast to the family she'd left behind.

The stench of the air had now settled in her throat, and she swallowed, trying to get the taste out of her mouth, to no avail. She had hardly remembered that her new father-in-law was there at all, until he stood, and placed a strike-a-light on the table before her. Agnes glanced up at his face and noticed with a start that he was smiling kindly at her. The relief was almost unbearable, and without warning, tears began to sting the back of her eyelids, threatening to spill onto her cheeks.

"Come now, Agnes, we'll all get along just fine. Silo is upset about the display at the feast, but you are not the first child of spring to do that, and you will not be the last. He forgets that you have a lifetime to make each other smile. Ah, my own wife on our wedding day, why she wasn't sure about marrying a tanner either.

But you get used to the smell. Here, light the fire and clear the kitchen. Make it your own. We are happy to have you." With a nod, he straightened up and headed for the door, wrapping his own leather apron about his stomach. He turned once there and looked back. "You can call me Pa, if you wish. It's no hardship."

As the door closed behind him, Agnes let out a sob. Kindness. Kindness in her new home. It was more than she had hoped for, and perhaps, maybe, she could live a life with Silo if her father-in-law was there to offer sweet words.

*

The light faded quickly once Agnes was left alone. The first thing she did was survey the scene before her. The dirt was ingrained into the wood as though it had been months since it was touched. Agnes stepped outside to fetch a bucket of water, the first of a lifetime of trips. The men were nowhere to be seen. She paused, hearing the faint laughter and music of the feast, and wished dearly that she were there. Instead, the waterwheel turned with great whooshes and creaks, the sound of her new existence.

Once back indoors, Agnes got to work. She cleared and swept the floors, rinsed the plates and tankards, banished the food to the compost heap outdoors. She found wood at the back of the house and moved piles to beside the fire, dirtying her dress. She stacked new logs onto the flames, watching her hand move in and out with a little pleasure, playing with the fire as much as she liked. Her mother wasn't here to tell her no, now. Once done, she noticed the sun had set, and the room was barely light. The fire lit up the hearth, and not knowing where candles were kept, Agnes pulled up a chair in front of the fireplace, feeling the glow on her face as she peeled the turnips she had found beneath the table in a sack. They were old, their skin wrinkled and sprouting small arms, but they would do. Her mother had taught her this, and she would ensure that she had achieved her first task of married life:

to provide food. In truth, the scent of acrid, decaying flesh was so strong that the turnips would have a lot to contend with once on the tongue, but try she did.

When the sun had fully set in the sky, and Agnes could no longer see out of the windows, the door creaked open. The smell became stronger immediately, a stench that made her toes curl and body flinch, but she tried her best to welcome the men. She stood, brushing the creases from the front of her dress, the words she had planned all afternoon sticking in her throat.

"Good evening, I hope work was—"

"Why is it so dark?" Silo said immediately, pulling a stool roughly from beneath the table.

"I did not know—" Agnes began, wanting to explain that she wasn't sure where the candles were, that she didn't know whether it was right to light one.

"We are not destitute, Agnes. We are not paupers. We can afford to eat by the light of a candle or two." Silo's voice was strained and clipped, as though the events of earlier that day were weighing heavily on him still. A silence followed.

"Of course, Silo, I didn't know where they were kept," Agnes eventually said, rage bubbling up her windpipe and threatening to blister into her mouth. She swallowed it down.

Pa sighed, a hearty breath that told Agnes he was not as angry, and pulled a drawer open beneath the table. He selected a couple of candle sticks and their holders, placed them on the table, and lit them with the strike-a-light. When done, he sat back in a larger chair and closed his eyes. Agnes quickly plated up the turnips and placed them on the table. Her stomach was begging for food, cloying for attention.

"How grateful we are for our food today, how we thank the Gods for gifting us with such blessing. We welcome Agnes into this house with the knowledge that she will try her best. Gods, enable her to do better, to strive for the life we expect of her. We thank you," Silo said loudly. A murmur came from Pa, who repeated the last line. There was an uncomfortable pause in the room, and Agnes cleared her throat.

"We thank you," she said. It was very different from the grace that her mother and father had taught her to say, with no nods to the bounty of the Gods or the kingdom which graced them. In silence, they ate. When the eating was done, it was time for the part of the wedding day Agnes knew nothing about.

*

It was rare to have a separate bedroom in Locklear, or indeed, across the land. Space inside was at a premium, and Agnes had expected to share a room with both men. At home, she had shared a room with her brother, once, and the gift he had given her by leaving was only one of space.

When Silo showed her into their room, the first thing she saw was the new wall that had been built as a divide. It touched her heart, this indication of planning, of caring and forethought. She would share a room with her husband, as she expected, but not with Pa. The second thing she saw was the bed, narrow and wooden, much like her own at home. And then, with interest, she saw a strange, deep leather chair in the corner of the space.

She had never seen anything like it. It was so at odds with the wooden stools of home. Home. A strange word that stuck in her mind. This was her home now—she mustn't forget.

"Sit down," Silo said, "try it."

Agnes accepted, her limbs tired from the long day, her skin excited to feel something that looked so luxurious against it. She sat. The leather was unlike that of her father's apron, different from her brother's hard boots. It was like butter, running across the back of her thighs.

"It is your wedding present," Silo muttered as though it were a gift he did not wish to bestow. Agnes nodded, touching the careful sewing upon the arm. It was glorious, beyond what she could have hoped for. She glanced up at the man she had married that day and tried a smile. He barely looked at her, focusing instead on his craftsmanship, which Agnes admitted was very fine.

"Thank you, Silo. I am grateful to you. I am...I am sorry about today."

At the mention of this, Silo held up his hand and shook his head.

"If you are not awake by the time the first cockerel crows, then you have overslept." With those words spoken, he climbed into bed.

Agnes stayed in the chair. He had made her a wedding present. It was something she hadn't expected, a kindness unaccounted for. Still in her grey wedding dress, she stood and moved towards the bed. She pulled back the covers and slid in, feeling the rough linen against her legs. Silo blew out the candle, and Agnes closed her eyes, trying to imagine that she was in her bed at home, that this new smell wasn't wrapping her tightly in its grip.

After a moment, she heard Silo sigh, and she felt him move next to her. Her brother had told her about something once, and she remembered now. He had told her that when she was married, something would be expected that no one ever spoke about, and it was how you had children.

"Agnes," Silo said, his breath thick in the darkness.

"Yes?"

"Have you ever...?" The question lingered, and while Agnes didn't know exactly what he was referring to, she knew that she hadn't.

"No."

There was a pause.

"Me neither." With a hesitant hand, Silo reached for her. In barely a moment, the deed was supposedly done, and neither said any more about it. Agnes let herself relax, tried to fall asleep, her body bone weary, the place between her legs sore. She was a wife now, she knew.

Chapter Eight

By the time the cockerel first crowed, Agnes was in the kitchen preparing the fire. She had barely slept, the foreign noises of the house creaking around her, the odd movements of Pa in the next room, coughing and snoring and huffing. The scent of her husband beside her was strange, a lingering hint of sweat beneath the urine, a smell she could not quite place: husband. With care, she lit the fire, placing the logs inside, watching her fingers dance across the flame.

"Careful, child, you'll burn yourself."

Agnes pulled back quickly, wiping her hands on the apron she had found under the table. She turned to see Pa, pipe in mouth, shuffling into the kitchen.

"It's good advice. Here, sit, I'll make porridge." Agnes smiled and poured the prepared oats and water into the cauldron, pushing it over the fire.

"You slept well?" Pa asked.

"Not really, no." There was something about him, something warm, that made Agnes feel as though she could truly be honest. He nodded, huffing into his pipe.

"It's strange being at a new house. My wife found it the same. It's a bit like having her back, you being here. I was lying in bed listening to you potter around the kitchen, and it was just...like having her back."

Agnes smiled, selected a wooden spoon and stirred the porridge. She thought of her mother and how she would be doing the same thing around now, preparing food for her father's breakfast.

"What was her name?" Agnes asked.

"Violet."

Silo walked into the room, head down, and sat heavily at the table. His eyes were tired, bleary, and he said nothing.

"Porridge, Silo?" Agnes tried, offering him a smile. She wanted there to be some warmth there, a little slice of home. There had to be. If she couldn't create what her mother had, she would fail. He raised his eyes to her and nodded.

"And hopefully," Pa carried on talking as though there had been no pause, "we will have another little one around here soon. We need to carry on the family business, Agnes, so we'll need a strong lad. So just you make sure that you're keeping up your end of the bargain, and all will be well."

Silo accepted the bowl that Agnes was handing him, and they caught eyes for a moment. Agnes searched them. What was there? Agreement? Hope? Despair? She couldn't read them at all. Children. A strong lad. Another mouth, another hard stare accepting porridge.

"Do you hear what Father is saying, Agnes?" Silo said suddenly, pulling Agnes from her thoughts. She nodded, ladling out more porridge into a bowl. She heard, but the thought of it made her stomach ache. A child within the walls of her body, growing and pushing out her skin. She couldn't help but think of the hides she had seen outside, hanging in the sun, the fur stripped from them. Perhaps he was already in there, this strong lad, moving her muscles and bones to make room for himself. Bile bubbled in her throat, and she swallowed it down. She would become a tanner's wife from the inside out, bare flesh waiting to dry in the sun.

*

Once the men had gone, Agnes sat at the table and ate her own breakfast. She thought of Saskia, of what she might be doing now, and how Finn would be eating his breakfast. Their house must smell of honey and mint, she thought, of joy and sunshine. Within an instant, she had made up her mind. Yesterday already seemed like so long ago, and without a friend in this world, Agnes was bound to this house. She had to apologise, to make amends. The women who pushed against the walls of the town were destined to be punished.

Agnes changed into one of the three dresses she now owned. Her wedding dress had been put away in the old chest that was her dowry, she supposed, in case she had a daughter, and her work dress was now interlaced with the scents of a tanner's wife. She pulled out the only other dress, a dark brown canvas one that her mother had made for the winter months. The weather was too warm for it, and so she knew that this would look strange, but to show up at Saskia's house in either of the other two would not do. Once ready, she stared about the kitchen desperately, hoping that there would be something, anything to gift to Saskia as an apology. To start married life with a debt was embarrassing, and although Silo hadn't said as much, it was clear that he and Finn were some sort of friends. After all, they had been together when they had first met at the tavern. There was nothing to give them aside from some rat droppings and cold porridge. Wildflowers would have to do.

*

Agnes arrived at Saskia's door with a bunch of yellow daffodils in hand, sweating beneath the thick dress. Though she could not feel the heat, her skin still reacted to the weather. For Agnes, warmth meant the feeling of damp sweat, and cold of prickling skin. The thought of seeing Saskia and Finn was making her body twitch with embarrassment. As she hesitantly lifted her hand to knock on the door, it swung open.

"What do you want?" Saskia's mother stood, her hands on her slim hips. She was wearing a light green gown, something that Agnes couldn't have kept clean for a second, and her hair was long and silver, trailing around her middle like a rope of silken braid.

She looked Agnes up and down and then pulled her clean hand to her nose. "Goodness me, Agnes, you have the smell of a tanner's wife already. Step back, will you? Those flowers aren't helping a bit."

Agnes obeyed, stepping backwards from the step into the mud behind her.

"Is Saskia here?"

"No," her mother answered, folding her arms. There was silence.

"Oh...I had hoped to make my apologies." Agnes bowed her head to show that she was truly aiming for an act of contrition. Her heart beat against her skin, and she felt it more keenly than usual. The apology wasn't real, Agnes knew. She had apologised before, to her brother, when she had shoved him too hard in play and he had hurt his foot. That was a real apology: sorrowful, tender, desperate. This felt different. Agnes felt a twinge of irritation, the same uncomfortable wince of unfairness she had experienced the day before.

"And I should think so. I should think so. Well, she and her husband, with no thanks to you, have moved in right over the square there. Prime position, I'm sure you would agree, especially for a first home. Not even I had such a first home."

Agnes nodded, following the woman's slender finger over the road, where a wooden cottage stood. The front window boxes were brimming with daffodils, practically glowing yellow against the clean whitewash, and Agnes suddenly felt her cheeks flush red as though she had picked her flowers from their very garden. By the time she had turned back, the door had closed in her face.

Agnes crossed the square with purpose, trying to look as though she were proud of herself. This, she realised, was the way she thought wives carried themselves after their wedding day, chin high and shoulders back, as if they were now a citizen of the world, and no longer a child. As she came within the vicinity of Saskia's door, it opened. A young woman stood, eyes wide, tying her apron behind her back.

"Yes, ma'am?" she asked, giving a slight bob of the knees. Agnes could see her nose twitch. They had a maid. How many other wives in the town had maids?

"I would like to see Saskia, please."

"And you are...?"

Agnes paused. If she said her name, she might be turned away. She already felt as though her back and ears itched with the words of the neighbours, as though they were all watching her.

"A friend."

The maid was too young to know what to do in this situation, and Agnes could see it. A more experienced housekeeper might have held her ground, but this one stepped aside and led Agnes through the hallway to a strange room holding only chairs. She indicated that she should sit and then left her alone. Agnes had never seen anything like this—a room to sit in? There was no hearth, just space. A few books were spread across a table, and then her eyes rested on a chair, just like her own at home. Her wedding present. Perhaps they had commissioned one for their wedding, too.

"You're joking," came Saskia's voice as she suddenly appeared in the doorway. She was wearing white, still, although a different dress from the day before. Such luxury Agnes could not imagine. Her face was grim, pale. As with her mother, her hand flew up to her nose. "So, you're a tanner's wife. You smell like a tanner's wife. I could smell you from upstairs."

"Saskia, I came to apologise." Agnes held up the flowers with a tired smile, trying, really trying, to make an effort. "I don't know what I was—"

"Oh, I know what you were thinking, Agnes. I know exactly what you were thinking. You were thinking that my betrothed was better than yours, and you're right. But why, Agnes, do you think that is?" Saskia moved into the room, her body swaying with contempt. She pinched her nostrils together with her long fingers, looking down on her unwanted guest. Agnes felt the words coming, battling to crawl out of the woman's pert mouth.

"It's because I am better than you. You are destined to be a tanner's wife. That's what you are. Embrace it. I hear Silo and his pop are expecting children, quick smart, so you better get on home now, eh? Lots to do in that old house, all by yourself." She paused, stepping back a little and glancing around her as though making sure no one else was there. "Just mind the rafters."

Agnes breathed in sharply, not understanding and trying to get a scent of that honey but failing. It was true; she took up all the smells in the room. She stood, taking the daffodils with her.

"These are not from your front, by the way. Best of luck, Saskia. I have apologised. I have done my part. May you and yours be blessed by the Gods." She bowed her head and pushed past the golden girl, heading for the front door. As she left, she heard Saskia's final words.

"We are blessed, Agnes. And you, are cursed."

Chapter Nine

By the time she arrived home, the sun was dipping slightly in the sky. Agnes was still clutching the daffodils, and she pushed them into a cup, placing them in the centre of the table. She looked around. None of the chores that she had intended to be done that morning, sweeping the floors upstairs and down, batting the dust out of the rugs and bed sheets, prepping the fire and food, had been completed. With a grimace, she pulled her apron on and began to peel turnips, taking each with a rough hand. What did Saskia mean when she said that she was cursed? The mere mention of such a word seeped into her bones, as though it were part of her body. To be cursed would be an awful sin. Surely, the golden girl did not know about her blessing, her gift with flame?

"Agnes." There was a footstep on the stairs.

"Yes?"

No answer. Wiping her hands on a cloth, Agnes rounded her shoulders. It would be her husband, no doubt, or his father, ready to take her to task about the fact that food was not ready. In fact, she knew it was late, though goodness knows how long they had been home and waiting. Her cheeks stung with embarrassment. Hesitantly, she climbed the steps, her nostrils smarting with the dry scent of ammonia. First, she checked her bedroom. Her husband was not there, and so she knew it must have been his father. She moved next door quickly, checking. He wasn't there either.

"Agnes." The voice came again. It was coming from downstairs now, and hastily, Agnes hurried down the steps, her boots flicking mud off her feet as she stepped, leaving marks behind on the wood. The kitchen, too, was empty. At that, the main door swung open. Silo and his father trooped in, and Pa looked at the lonely turnip peeled on the side.

"Let's hope that's for dinner and that lunch is prepared. You've had ample time," Pa said, his dirtied brow furrowing.

Agnes shook her head. "I am sorry, I have been out in town today and have not yet had time to make the lunch. It took longer than I—"

"Agnes," Silo said, the word falling from his mouth with such disinterest that it shocked her. She replayed the voice that had said her name just moments previously and couldn't see that it belonged to anyone here. "Agnes," he said again, as though he knew her mind was wandering. He stepped forward and plucked a daffodil from the cup, crushing it beneath his fingers.

"We cannot eat flowers. This is the first and the last time I expect this to happen. Unless it is market day, you have no business in town. Come, Father," he turned to Pa, his face away from Agnes so she could not see his expression, "I shall take you to the tavern for a pint and a pie. The Gods know we have earned the break."

The pair left, the door shutting behind them, and Agnes was left standing in the kitchen, her mouth open. A pint and a pie was a luxury she had never seen her father enjoy. But then, hadn't her mother always prepared lunch for him, right on time? She tried to imagine it before her, a pint and a pie, surely a cost that a small household such as this could not afford. How was it that she was scouring turnips that were growing their own siblings, and the men were able to go out in such a way?

"Agnes." The voice again came clear and fast, and Agnes wasn't sure if it was a thought or an actual voice that spoke to her. In silence, she picked up another turnip and began peeling for dinner.

*

That night, after the fire had blazed and the three had eaten before it, Agnes climbed into bed beside her husband. This time, the act lasted longer, the noises were louder, and his breath soured with the scent of ale. As he rolled over, taking much of the blanket with him, he sighed a few words.

"You better provide us with that son soon, Agnes. Pa is getting old."

The words bounced around her mind as she listened to his breath slow, and she felt a damp stickiness spread between the tops of her thighs. To hold a baby, what would that be like? To have a baby in this house. She had known others in the village with children, of course, had heard many birthing stories. They were horrific, rarely beautiful. She had seen the women grow, skin and stomachs stretching before the Grothi, supposedly blessed by each step. Some of the women had died. Some of the babies had died before and after birth, and the women been dragged into the forest, hung for their sins. Agnes wrapped her arms around herself in the hot air and breathed in the scent. Perhaps one day, that smell would be a comfort to her, but not now. Now, it pulled her deep into the bed, suffocating her with its tendrils, digging into her throat and dragging bile up into her mouth. Agnes gasped, pushing herself up onto her forearms, struggling for breath. She let out a silent scream.

Chapter Ten

Sunday came in a whirl of cleaning. Agnes looked back on her week with a strange type of disgust. After it had been made clear to her that market day was the only day on which she should leave the house, and then on the market day, she had been told there was no spare money for the food that week, she found herself bouncing between the wooden walls of the kitchen. Every day had been like the one before it. Every night meant the same thing. Silo had barely looked her in the eyes the entire week, and when he had, it was with such a glare that she had wanted to apologise. As with the other days, she had woken up early, before the cockerel crowed. She was sure the men wouldn't be working today but wasn't sure what that meant for their plans. Nerves settled in her stomach, flickering beneath her skin like a bolt of lightning.

She prepped the fire, made the breakfast, and waited. Both men were late to come down, and when they eventually did, Silo grumbled about the texture of his oats, craggy to the touch. After eating, Agnes picked up the bucket to collect water from the stream and felt a firm hand on her arm.

"It is Sunday, Agnes. We must go to the Grothi for the protection ceremony. Leave the water until later. It does not matter as much as our dying souls," Silo said. Agnes nodded, putting the bucket back down. Nothing had been mentioned all week about this and so she had thought that the family wouldn't partake in the ceremony. Her family certainly didn't always partake, as much as they revered the Gods.

Agnes dressed carefully in her only smart dress, the wedding dress she had worn the week before, and braided her hair. The men met her by the door, and they left together, Agnes stepping behind the entire way. As they walked, she watched them speak in low whispers, their voices riding on the wind of their strong smell. Agnes could see that it was another warm day, relying as she often did on the dimples in the air, the heat mirage. Despite this, Agnes had chosen to bring a woollen shawl with her. The people of the town would be watching her, and she knew to be afraid. Her behaviour the week before was shameful, and she was clearly not yet forgiven. She could only hope that if her mother and father were there, they would speak to her.

*

The protection ceremony took place every Sunday (except for the day of the Spring Feast) and the girls of spring were placed front and centre. This was where Agnes had always sat, but now, things were different. Now, she was a wife. As they stepped inside the wooden building, their feet muddied from the long walk, Silo paused and uttered something to his father. Pa walked on, and Silo dropped back, offering his arm to Agnes. A strange event, and yet Agnes took it, grateful for a sign of forgiveness. He glanced at her and moved a little closer as they stepped.

"Say nothing to Finn and Saskia, Agnes. What is done is done, and the best you can do for both of us is to reclaim your dignity."

Agnes nodded. He was right, of course, and she had humiliated him. The humiliation of a husband was surely not so easy to forgive. The people of the congregation were about them, stepping in time, some holding their wives' arms, others striding ahead. Agnes searched the people desperately for her mother and father, praying that today would be the day they chose to attend. No luck. They weren't anywhere in sight. Perhaps she had embarrassed them so much that they felt they couldn't bear to be in the same place as her for a time, that they wanted to let the distance reduce what they had in common with her.

Agnes let her eyes fall on the paintings of the Gods, who stared out from murals that adorned the walls. Their large eyes followed wherever you went, watching, knowing. As a child, she had found them terrifying. As an adult, she was still afraid. One in particular always filled her with fear, his cream cloak billowing behind him, a red crown perched atop his head. His gaze was hard, a heavy brow. He looked as though he knew every part of you.

"Wives, won't you join me on this side," the Grothi said loudly, his voice booming through the long wooden room as they stepped inside.

Agnes let go of Silo's arm, walking to the front of the church alongside the other women. Small steps, trying not to be seen, knowing that she could be smelled. Saskia glanced at her, her eyes sharp and foreboding, and stepped before her. The scent of honey once more wafted under Agnes' nostrils, and she noticed that she too was wearing her dress from last week, hair laden with yellow flowers, air as light as summer. In comparison, Agnes felt strange and heavy, her legs being forced in front of her, a dull light, an extinguished flame. They lined up before the Grothi. Agnes had watched this many times and never with much attention. She knew what was going to come, though.

"And so, as we welcome the new wives in the first week of matrimony, we say goodbye to the dead." With a wave of his heavily robed arm, the Grothi stepped forward. A few young men began to walk up the middle aisle, carrying two large and long boxes on their shoulders. They placed the dead on the opposite side of the wives, and the Grothi bowed his head.

"The Gods know that a town the size of ours cannot survive with more mouths to feed, and so they bless us with the loss at the same time as the giving. Two have died since the marriage of our young wives, to be replaced by two babes in nine months. Daughters of the Gods, if you know that it is you of whom I speak, step forward."

Agnes hesitated. How could she possibly know? She didn't want it to be her. Was that enough? Her breath caught in her throat, and she swallowed. Beside her, Saskia stepped forward, leaving a trail of her glorious scent behind, almost visible to the eye. After a moment, another woman stepped forward at the end of the line, and Agnes exhaled a long breath of relief. How they knew, she couldn't guess, but she was grateful that it wasn't her. With a sickness building in her throat, she hoped it never would be. She imagined Finn behind them in the crowd, his smile flourishing, shoulders relaxed. Silo, on the other hand, would remain still and silent, his humiliation complete.

"Bless you, our daughters, our wives, for you have already proven yourselves to be one of us," the Grothi said, placing a hand on each woman's shoulder. He glanced at Agnes, his dark eyes old and weary, and she noticed an almost imperceptible shake of the head.

"The rest of you must try harder."

Had she ever listened to his words before, in the years gone by? Surely, they had never been so cruel. And yet her mind had been full of other things as she sat in the seats, waiting to go home. Her thoughts had been full of the hopes of spring, the warm weather that awaited her. The thought of going home to her brother, playing in the stream, digging her hands into the burning flame of the furnace and forging her own sword. Though she had occasionally heard the screams of the women in the trees at night, her mother had always told her not to worry. Such thoughts had never entered her mind in church before. But now, she felt the heavy gaze of the Grothi and knew that she needed to correct her error.

The wives were dismissed, and Agnes, palms clammy, went and took a seat beside Silo. He didn't look at her. The Grothi continued.

"The kingdom has sent a message to all the Grothi on this fine spring morning to remind us that the war at the border of our land continues. Do not worry, my friends, for they are far away, and the King and Queen are protecting you. We have our own blacksmith forging for the effort, and our people are doing their utmost to keep the barbarians at bay. And be under no illusion—they are barbarians. They want a world without their royalty, divined by the Gods. If you can imagine such a world, then picture a scene of fire and ruin, from which there is no return."

Agnes thought of her brother again, of his leaving. Would he be on the battlefield now, holding a sword made by their father, without realising it? With a sharp sting in her heart, she realised that it was just as likely that he was dead, lying in a ditch along the path to the kingdom.

Chapter Eleven

"I would like to visit my mother, Silo, for she was not at church." The words swam through the air, and Silo watched them as they landed before him.

"Do as you need, but you must be home in time for lunch," he said. Agnes nodded, though apparently not enthusiastically enough. "Agnes. Do you understand?"

"Yes," she responded, glancing up at him. His eyes were sunken into his head, the bags beneath low and dark. With a slight dip of the knee and a bow of the head, Agnes turned and walked the familiar path back to her real home, pretending that it was at least the month before, that she was no longer a wife.

She could smell the furnace from yards away. The smoke billowed into the air as it always had, and the shape of her father came into view quickly. She stepped with enthusiasm, excited to see him and to watch as he toiled, playing with the metal, shaping the swords. "Father!"

He paused, turned, and looked behind him. His expression wasn't what she had hoped, not the face-splitting smile or the relieved laugh. He simply watched her come closer while weighing the hammer in his hand.

"Father, you were not at church. I have come to see how you are," Agnes said as she came within earshot. Her father nodded, wiping his brow, and turned back to the furnace.

"I have had another order from the kingdom and shall be taking on an apprentice. I must make sure that there are enough tools to share with him from tomorrow, and so, there is work to be done."

As he spoke, the door to the small homestead opened. The scent of her mother's cooking emerged from the space, and Agnes breathed it in as though it had been years since she had smelled it last.

"Daughter. You smell like a tanner's wife," her mother said, raising a handkerchief to her nose.

"We cannot all marry blacksmiths, apparently," Agnes shot back. Her mother was the one who had chosen Silo as her mate, not her. She should have guessed the scent that would follow.

"You have news?" Her mother's voice was taut with expectation as she paused at the threshold, her body a barrier rather than a welcome. The unspoken question hung in the air: would she not invite her own daughter in?

Agnes swallowed hard. "No, no news. I came to see why you did not attend church."

"And you come alone. No husband?"

"No," Agnes said.

"Well, we did not attend church for many a reason." Her mother's voice was brittle, each word carefully measured. "Your father has a lot to do by tomorrow, and our daughter did, unfortunately, shame us at the Spring Feast. We shall wait until all is forgotten unless you have news."

Agnes felt the weight of rejection settling on her shoulders. No warm embrace awaited her here, no comforting cup of soup. If she could turn back time to a week ago, perhaps she would choose differently. But that option was as closed to her as her childhood home now seemed.

"What news would you hope for, Mother?" The words tumbled from Agnes' lips before she could stop them, bitter and sharp. "That I would be leaving town? Following in my brother's footsteps?" The instant the words left her mouth, Agnes recognised her mistake. Her mother glared, her father glowered.

"Agnes," he said roughly, a large chunk of metal in his hand, glowing red from the fire, "come back when you are with child. Until then, leave us to create peace. Forgiveness is not so easily given."

His words pricked at her skin like the sharp end of a sword. Agnes nearly laughed aloud, disbelief coursing through her veins. He had never spoken to her in this way, never delivered news with such a blunt edge. In silence, Agnes turned away from her former home, the giddy anticipation of seeing her family now a hollow ache in her chest.

*

The path back to the tanner's house—her new home—seemed longer than before. Agnes' mind raced, searching for ways to bridge the chasm that had opened between her and her family. A child, it seemed, was the only currency that might buy her way back into the fold.

Her hand drifted half-heartedly to her stomach. Could the Gods see beneath her dress? Did they know what lay within? The Grothi had always been clear: the giving of a child was a blessing. Agnes watched the mud underfoot, soft in the heat, and felt it squash around her thin leather boots. Why didn't it feel like a blessing?

How had Saskia and that other woman known? The women of the village had never spoken of such things, and her mother had never shared these secrets. How did one discern these matters without dabbling in witchcraft?

Her feet turned as if without direction, and she found herself following the path up to Saskia's homestead, just off the main square. Silo wouldn't be expecting her back so soon; he would assume she was still with her parents, basking in familial warmth. The irony of that thought was not lost on her.

As she neared Saskia's front door, her palms grew damp with nervous anticipation. She had to know. The scent of daffodils and sight of the yellow flowers danced before her. It was almost dazzling, the sunshine that seemed to push from the window. Joyful. She knocked without hesitation; she had nothing to lose.

This time, there was no maid to open the door. Saskia pulled it open with a low gaze, recoiling at the sight.

"I could smell you were coming," she said, stepping backwards slightly. "What do you want?"

Agnes moved forward. She was a tanner's wife; they would need to get used to it. "Saskia, I have to know how you knew about...your..." She indicated to her stomach, eyes wide.

Saskia let out a laugh, the tinkling noise ringing in Agnes' ears. "Because I know. When you know, you know."

"But how?" Agnes pushed.

"Didn't your mother ever teach you anything?"

Agnes shook her head. "Please, Saskia. I won't bother you again. I need help."

"After this, find yourself help from Widow Sewall. She is far more your...level. Get some wheat seeds before they are sewn. Urinate on them. It smells like you piss all over your clothes anyway, so that shouldn't be hard for you. When they sprout, you're with child." The door slammed in Agnes' face as quickly as she opened her mouth to respond. Wheat seeds. Wheat seeds were the answer. On the way home to make lunch, Agnes stopped by the bakery to make the purchase.

Chapter Twelve

Once lunch was eaten and the fire built, Agnes waited until the men had settled by the hearth, both gently closing their eyes. She could see that this was the rhythm of their Sunday, restful and godly. It was not hugely unlike that of her childhood, albeit her father often worked throughout.

Agnes took herself outside with the bucket, pretending to need water. She headed beyond the stream towards the cesspit and paused once there. Carefully, she pulled her handkerchief from her pocket and placed the wheat seeds on top of it. She then put it on the floor and knelt over it, urinating onto the cloth. Once done, she wrapped it up, placed it gently in her pocket, and collected the water she needed.

How long would it take? She had no idea. Perhaps it was a nightly thing, and she would open the cotton kerchief the next day to find sprouting. If so, she would tell Silo and Pa, and their anger would dissipate, allowing her to breathe in the house. She could tell her parents, and they would wrap their arms around her, pulling her back into the fold.

As she entered the house once more, she found only Silo sitting by the fire. Agnes put the bucket down and sat beside her husband. She thought of saying the three words to him, just to see his reaction. What would he do? It would mean that tonight she would be able to rest, to sleep, without worrying. She didn't want the result; she couldn't see her way to having the actual child, but she wanted the fact. Nine months of safety, that's what the Grothi had meant. Silence fell between the two, and Agnes opened her mouth.

"On the way home from my parent's house, I visited the bakery."

Silo opened his eyes and glanced at her, shaking his head. "My mother would bake her own bread. It is a needless expense."

"No, I didn't buy bread. I bought wheat seeds," Agnes began, reaching into her pocket to pull out the kerchief. Silo raised a hand silently.

"Please, women's troubles are not something you should draw a husband into. When you are certain, tell me then."

Agnes paused, pushing the damp cloth back into the folds of her dress. Of course, she wasn't sure now what she had been thinking, trying to show him. There was something that she had hoped, a sort of closeness that might come with her showing willingness. But inside, she was not willing. She was sour. Beneath her feet, the soil and the rotting floorboards waited, and she felt the heartbeat of the children she would never bear.

*

In the middle of the night, Agnes opened her eyes. She needed the toilet. She listened to the animals outside the house, the pawing and crowing and snuffling of danger. With care and quiet, she climbed out of the covers, trying not to wake her husband. There was a bucket beneath the bed for such an eventuality, but something told her to go out as she might in the day. With a silent step, she wrapped herself in her shawl and climbed down the stairs.

The fire was dying in the grate of the kitchen, the sound of snores from Pa's room filling the small house.

"Agnes." She heard the word as she reached for the door and paused. She turned. No one was there. Pa continued to snore, and the floorboards above hadn't creaked to signal her husband. With a breath, she stepped towards the fire, reaching in and grabbing a hot coal. She would take it with her for protection.

"Agnes." The voice again. It was light, almost indistinct, but it was there. She had no doubt. Her heart began to thump, thump, inside her ears, and she backed to the door, looking around.

"Sewall." The voice was louder this time, and Agnes turned, pushing open the door and fleeing into the night.

The moon was high and bright in the sky, providing a cool and welcoming blanket across the land. Agnes stepped onward, her bare feet crossing onto the damp grass by the stream, and breathed in the cold air of the nighttime. She closed her eyes for a moment. Calm. Let calm arrive. She knew she wasn't losing her mind; it was only the pressure of this new life. The pressure of change, the strangeness of the last weeks. Carefully, she removed the handkerchief from her pocket and spread it onto the ground once more, squatting over it. Afterwards, she looked at the seeds. No growth was shown there, nothing but seeds. She sucked in the air around her, tasting the job of her husband. She was relieved and strangely disappointed. She was both. Once finished, she pocketed the seeds again and walked back to the house. It wasn't lit in the same way her own home had once been. Her mother had always kept a candle outside the back at night so that she could find her way safely when needed. When her brother had left, she had blown it out. It seemed that it was no longer needed to guide errant children home.

Once back in the kitchen, Agnes pulled up a stool in front of the dying fire and replaced the coal. She was tired, her bones aching, but she didn't want to join Silo in their bed. She just wanted a moment to herself.

"Agnes." The voice again.

Quietly, she answered, "Yes?"

There was no response, but Agnes listened closely to the room about her. A strange, creaking noise was all that she could hear.

Chapter Thirteen

Market day. Agnes had looked forward to it, carefully putting aside the few coins that Silo had given her throughout the week. The last few days, she had purposefully squatted over her seeds every morning, and yet found no growth. Silo hadn't asked, not once. The air inside the house was still dank and unwelcoming, and despite Agnes' efforts to brighten the space with flowers and compliments, they fell on soundless responses.

"Will you be needing anything from the market, Silo, Pa?" Agnes asked as the men ate their breakfasts. Pa silently shook his head, and Silo glanced up at her.

"Be frugal, be fair. One piece of meat should suffice. Remember that we have the deal with the butcher."

Agnes nodded, relieved. She had been momentarily worried that he would tell her she couldn't go, even though she had already made up her mind that she would go anyway. When the men left, Agnes removed her apron, picking up the basket from beneath the table.

The walk there was blessed with sunshine, the day bright. The further Agnes walked from her home, the sweeter the air became. As scattered houses gave way to alleyways and bustling streets, Agnes found herself swept up in the growing crowds, her heart quickening with the hope of seeing her mother's face or catching a familiar smile.

The market was a regular staple of village life, and Agnes had always loved it. Perusing the stalls with her mother and brother had once been the best part of her week. Their ritual was etched in her memory: first, the vibrant displays of fruits and vegetables, then the aromatic offerings of the baker and butcher, before finally reaching the pinnacle of excitement, the craft stalls. There, amid leather strips, linens, and occasional furs, Agnes had always felt a world of possibilities unfurl before her. Sometimes, a wisher woman would come through town with a box full of trinkets and show them beads and pieces of thread, telling them how they could make jewellery to last their lives. Of course, her mother would never let her purchase these precious things. They were for the wealthier, her mother said, as Agnes watched Saskia add another rare bead to her bracelet.

Now, as a wife, Agnes felt the weight of her coin purse with newfound responsibility. Her mother's lessons on frugality echoed in her mind, though Agnes prided herself on her own sensible thinking. She couldn't purchase more than she had money for, so she needed to make sure she was careful and prepared. Meat, cabbage and milk were allowed. Anything else could be saved for next week.

With confidence, Agnes approached the butcher's stall. He gazed at her lazily and stepped forward, wiping his hands on his bloody apron.

"Where's your mother today? Haven't seen her in a few weeks."

"She's at home, I should imagine," Agnes replied. "I'm after a few chops of pork, please."

The butcher frowned and then shrugged, picking up some cuts and wrapping them in linen. "Here, that's all? We got some nice fish, and your father's a fan of fish. Wouldn't mind if you brought some home, I dare say."

Agnes reached for the pork and placed it in her basket, removing her purse and dropping some coins into the butcher's hand. "But my husband is not such a fan, sir, so I shall leave it for today." Whether or not Silo was a fan of fish, Agnes had no idea. And yet, there was something she loved about the sentence she had just said, a grown-up sort of sentence, a sentence that an adult would say.

"Agnes."

She looked at the butcher expectantly, but he had already begun to talk to somebody else, oblivious to her grown-up declaration. Agnes scanned the crowd for her mother's familiar face, finding only strangers.

"Agnes."

Shaking her head to dispel the phantom voice, she continued walking down the centre of the stalls. The vegetable stall was next, and Agnes selected a large cabbage, exchanging it for coin once more. She stared at the other vegetables on offer, her hand pausing over some of them. Should she indulge? Probably not, she mused, shifting her basket from one hip to the other.

"Sewall."

The word swam into her ears. She stared at the woman who was running the vegetable stall and leaned in, "Did you say Sewall?"

"What was that?" the woman said, pausing as she counted change.

"Sewall," Agnes repeated.

"Oh, the Widow Sewall? You'll find her out past Dunstable farm, just on the left. Can't miss her house, it's a disgrace. The Gods know her work, and they shame her for it. If you are heading that way, take her a cabbage. Tell her it's from me. I keep on her good side." With a shiftless reach, the vegetable seller selected a small one and handed it to Agnes. She almost opened her mouth to say that she wasn't going there, but here was another cabbage. She placed it in her basket and nodded, moving on. As she walked away, she wondered what was best. If she kept the cabbage, they would have more to eat, and upon seeing how much money was left, Silo would perhaps give her a quiet word of well done. If she took the cabbage to the Widow Sewall, she would be late. The choice was, therefore, simple.

*

"You're home." Silo's words drifted through the door, and he shuffled in, yawning widely. He hadn't slept well; Agnes had felt him toss and turn beside her, and despite their regular dalliance, they were no closer.

"Yes. Come, look what I got from the market, and see what bartering I did," Agnes said, her chin high. She was proud, pleased with her work as a wife. Mending that error, she knew. She held out her hand to show the change she still had, indicating the goods she had purchased. Silo nodded once, a singular indication that she had not done terribly.

"Fine, fine. You will find your way. Did you speak to anyone there?"

A strange question. Agnes shrugged. "The stall holders, of course."

Silo stared at her, waiting. It was as though he was expecting her to say something else, but she didn't know what.

"I shall make cabbage soup for supper."

"Fine," Silo said again, sitting down before the fire and closing his eyes. Agnes busied herself, cutting and chopping, until she heard the strange sound of an unanswered question hanging in the air. She turned to see Silo staring at her.

"Do you have any news, Agnes?" he asked, his eyelids heavy.

She sniffed, realising what it was that he was truly asking. With surprise, she also noticed that she no longer smelled the acrid scent of urine on everything. Perhaps she had truly become a part of the furniture.

"I don't have any news." Agnes swallowed. Had she wished she could have said something different? What would he have said if she produced the sprouting wheat? But no, nothing had grown. She may as well have thrown them in the stream. Perhaps he might have looked at her with joy, swept her up in an embrace, the way her father used to when he came home from a trip away. Is that what she wanted?

"A shame. I did not expect it to take so long."

The words nestled into the space between them, and Agnes felt it touch her heart. If this was what was expected of her, perhaps she ought to try harder. With hesitation, she opened her mouth.

"Oh, I misunderstood your question," she said. "Yes, yes, there is news."

Silo sat up suddenly, his eyes wide, a smile creeping across his face. "You are with child?"

Agnes nodded. Silo stood, walking towards her. He laid a kind hand on her arm and squeezed. It was perhaps the most intimate thing that had happened to her since they met.

"I am pleased," he said.

Agnes drew a shaking breath. What now?

Chapter Fourteen

What Agnes knew about childbirth and child-rearing was limited. It had been only a day since delivering the news to Silo, and now Pa knew as well. He sat opposite her and nodded, sipping his lukewarm oats from a wooden spoon.

"Now then, you need to bear a male. A female will do us no good in the tannery, just another mouth to feed."

Agnes sighed, sitting down before the fire. An overwhelming desire to reach in and show her power came over her, and she bridled against it, a horse fighting the bit.

"I don't know if I can control such things, Pa. It is fate, is it not?"

"It is not. Go, ask your mother, for she bore a male first."

Agnes nodded, thinking of her brother. It was the first time that he had been mentioned by her new family, and she wanted to jump on the opportunity to discuss him. She hesitated, knowing better.

"That's right, your mother will be able to give you more advice than we," Silo added, and Agnes realised that this was the most either had spoken to her since she had arrived. The humiliation had been lifted. "The Grothi may also help."

A silence descended for a moment, and Agnes swallowed. The lie was already out of hand, a moment's decision changing the course of her life.

"Or, if we really want to be certain—" Silo continued.

"No, Son." Pa raised his hand, as though he knew what was coming next.

"It is not—" Silo continued.

"It is against the Gods," Pa said finally, brushing him off.

Agnes stared at the two men, curious. "I shall go and visit my mother this morning," she said, wondering if she were to continue this lie. Last night was the first night that Silo had not moved to her side of the bed, and as little as Agnes knew, she understood that without this, there would be no child at all.

*

Agnes caught sight of her father's silhouette against the distant furnace, a familiar tableau etched in firelight. She watched as he wiped his brow, straightened his back, and then, sensing her presence, glanced in her direction. With all her heart, she wished to run forward into his arms, to be swept up as he had when she was a child. But no, that would not do. She was an adult now, a wife. Her mind filled in the blank that came after that, soon to be a mother. A lie.

"Father!" Agnes called. He lifted a hand, brief, his lips moving as though speaking to the house. The front door creaked open once more, revealing her mother, hands busy with her apron. As Agnes drew nearer, she steeled herself with a deep breath. The Grothi's teachings echoed in her mind. Lying to one's parents was a grievous sin. Yet, how else could she reclaim their love? How could she make them run down the hill to her, hold her hand? It was as if they had embarked on new lives, ones in which they had no children at all.

"I have news," Agnes said loudly, causing the pair to glance at each other. Was that hope that she saw in their gaze, or was she imagining things? The heat of the furnace began to glow as she arrived, and she smiled at the two, noting their lack of mirth in response.

"What news?" her mother asked, her tone guarded.

"I am with child," Agnes said, the lie falling from her lips with ease. There was a pause in the air, a sour moment when Agnes wondered if life would ever be the same again. A smile began to creep across her mother's face, and then her father's, and both laughed.

"You are?" her mother asked, joy seeping from her pores. Agnes nodded. A nod was less of a lie, a lie by omission, perhaps.

Her father stepped forward, fulfilling her unspoken wish. His large arms enveloped her, drawing her close. Agnes buried her face in his apron and breathed in, smelling the familiar scent of home. Flame and charcoal, sweat and hard work. Her mother squeezed her arm, and Agnes pulled back, looking at the pair.

"Well, you must come in, Agnes. I'll fix up some stew. There is much to talk about," her mother said softly, and with her words, Agnes shone. Home again.

*

Her father had gone back to work, and her mother had laid out a spread indeed: stew, freshly baked bread, cabbage soup, and even a small slice of cake that she had purchased from the market only the day before.

"It is the strangest thing. I never spend money on such things, as well you know, but something told me it would be needed. And here we are." She was speaking to Agnes as though the entire wedding day had never happened, as if her humiliation of the family had been forgotten. Agnes took a bite of the sweet cake and flushed with pleasure.

"So, you will be hoping for a boy."

Agnes nodded. In this make-believe world, she supposed she would.

"Or rather, your husband will be. Tanning is not an easy profession, and a boy will be a fine apprentice. A girl is just another mouth to feed." Her words mirrored those of her new family, and Agnes understood her place in the world in sharp contrast to her brother's. Now that he was gone, she had become just another mouth to feed. No wonder they had sought to get her married so quickly.

"But of course, the child will not be born in the spring, so you will not have to deal with blessings of that sort." Her mother's eyes shifted and hardened, and she leaned in, voice lowering, although no one else was there. "I trust you are keeping your blessing quiet from your new family, Agnes."

Agnes nodded once more.

"Good. Well, there are a few ways to ensure a male heir, and I would recommend them. The Grothi can give a blessing, but it is not as certain as...other methods. Come, you must listen closely and take what I say as between you and me. Not even your father must know."

From outside, Agnes could hear her father brandishing his tools, the heavy booms of hammer upon metal rendering him unable to hear. Her mother beckoned her closer, and Agnes leaned in.

"I am serious, Agnes."

"I understand. I have experience with keeping things hidden."

"You have perhaps heard of the Widow Sewall?"

Agnes thought of the cabbage that sat on her table in her new home, collecting the scents of a tanner's kitchen, waiting to be sliced. A stolen cabbage. She nodded.

"She can guarantee a male. Visit her, but make sure that no one sees you. Do it when the sun has fallen from the sky. Wear dark clothing. Tell not even your husband."

Agnes nodded, frowning slightly. "Is this how you came by my brother?"

Her mother nodded, opening her mouth to speak once more. At that, the door opened, and her father stepped in, hands blackened with soot. He reached across the table and selected a piece of the cake, placing it between his lips with a smile.

"Oh, what a feast we have here! A feast fit for my family. Mother, are you telling her she must eat more? You are eating for two now, Agnes, so eat as though it is the Spring Feast, and you shall have a fine boy, tall and strong like your father."

Agnes could have sworn that he paused between the last two words, as though he wanted to say 'brother'. What had happened with herself and why she had been born female, she didn't know. Perhaps her spring gift, the curse bestowed on her, was the payment for her brother. What cost would a male be to her own family? The reality of her situation swam into her mind, and she realised with a start that she had almost forgotten it. She was not actually with child, but perhaps the Widow Sewall could fix that, too.

Chapter Fifteen

Agnes could barely wait for Silo to fall asleep. She lay beside him, heart fluttering in her throat, threatening to choke her. Earlier that evening, he had glanced at her stomach while she moved about the kitchen, and then audibly wondered when she would begin to show. She had laughed, *too soon*, she had said. *Too soon, Silo.* For a moment, it had felt real, as though it was too soon, but it was promised. He had smiled at her, a genuine, I am pleased you are here, smile. It had felt like theirs was almost a real relationship.

Silo's breath had now deepened, the soft squeak of his nostrils playing tunefully as he drew air in. After a moment, Agnes pulled back the sheets and quickly dressed. Her mother had told her which house was Widow Sewall's, and Agnes had memorised it. It was out of town, even further than the tannery was. Past Dunstable farm, as the woman at the market had said. Agnes had never been past Dunstable farm and had only been to its threshold a few times in her youth. There was nothing there, so what had she to gain? As for the Widow Sewall, whether or not she knew her already, she wasn't sure. There were plenty of older women in the village, some with the respected title of Widow, though Agnes had never had the need to call on them previously. The unremarkable was rarely remarked upon.

Agnes left the house and took her basket with her. She thought that if she came upon anyone in the street, she might tell them that she was out collecting verbena with a view to boiling it into tea to aid Pa with his sore joints. As she walked beneath the moon, she spotted the plant growing on a sharp slope under a tree and gently collected some, placing it into her basket. Her alibi was complete.

There was no one awake. Nobody appeared to stir as she walked through town, and it felt as though no eyes but the Gods' rested on her. Would the Widow be awake? Might Agnes irritate her with her presence? As she turned the corner to Dunstable farm, she saw, for the first time, that the path did indeed trickle beyond the old farmhouse. Up in the distance, there was a soft glow of light, and Agnes breathed in slowly. She was awake then.

The market stall owner had said that the house was a disgrace, and the closer that Agnes came, the more she understood this. The wooden slats of the house were corroding, the glow of the light peeping through cracks and holes in a way her father never would have allowed. It was clear that the straw on the roof hadn't been changed in many years, and even in the moonlight, Agnes could see it was rotting beneath the weight of the winter rains. As she stepped closer still, the light became brighter, and the old wooden door creaked open. There stood the silhouette of the Widow Sewall.

"Agnes," her voice was craggy and confident as if she expected her. "You have brought my cabbage with you?"

Agnes hesitated, swallowing. She couldn't quite make out the face of the Widow, but her stance hinted at age. She was stooped, her shoulders rounded in.

"I—um...cabbage?"

"Yes, the cabbage you were given in the market that you took home to your husband, the tanner. You have brought it?"

Agnes shook her head. "I have not. I apologise, I didn't realise—"

"You didn't realise I knew. And yet, you have brought verbena. A strange substitution. Still, what's done is done. Come in and mind the step." The Widow backed into the house, stepping aside, and Agnes nodded, clutching the handle of her basket in a clammy hand. She entered the small building, no more than a hut, and was hit with the strange scent of fish and firewood almost immediately.

"You certainly smell like a tanner's wife," the Widow said, closing the door behind her. Agnes bowed her head in silent apology and glanced around the room. It was bare, simple, with a similar fireplace and seat in front of it as in her own kitchen. A modest bed was made up in the corner. The only true difference from the other houses she had visited was the books, which filled the walls. The towers of them almost swayed, and Agnes stared. She could read, when needed. But really, there was never any need.

"Sit before the fire. The stool is for guests," the Widow said, seating herself in the armchair beside her. The air played with the warmth, and though Agnes could not feel it, she saw it filled the room.

Agnes sat, looking finally at the Widow's face in the firelight. She was younger than she had expected, the skin around her features craggy, yes, but bright. The woman smiled and spread her hands, palms upward, on her lap.

"Tell me why you have come."

Agnes paused. She had half expected the Widow to tell her why she was here. Should she be open about her reasoning? Were there formalities to adhere to?

"I...my mother said that you might be able to assist me in—"

"Hmm, yes. Bearing a son. This is what all of the women your age come to me for, in the dead of night, as though a son is the only thing worth having. And yet, you are not with child."

Agnes breathed in sharply, the air getting caught in her throat. "How do you know?"

"I can tell," the Widow replied, giving a small shake of the head. "You are not with child, and so you visit me tonight for something else."

"I do—" Agnes began, wringing her hands in her lap. "I do wish to be with child."

There was a silence in the air, and it crackled with strange anticipation.

"I find that a strange sentence, as your eyes tell me something different."

Agnes bit her cheek, feeling an irritation rise in her throat. She wanted to sigh, to kick, like a child. She wanted to stand up and shout, ask her what she should do to get back into her family's good graces if it weren't a baby. There were no other options.

"You are angry," the Widow Sewall said, her eyes glistening. Agnes nodded. "Yes, children come all too easy for some, but not so for others." With a steady hand, the old woman reached out across the flame of the fire and selected the handle of the steaming pot there. She picked up a worn cup from beside her and poured liquid into it, then passed it over. Agnes took it, smelling a strong and strange minty foulness coming from the brew.

"Drink this; it will make you feel a little better. It is tea, that is all," the Widow said, a small smile playing on her lips.

Agnes lifted the cup to her mouth and took a sip on command, feeling the thickness of flavour linger across her tongue. She swallowed; it was barely palatable.

"I would like to be with child, and it must be soon. What can you do for me?" Agnes asked.

"You do not wish for a spring child? You are too early if so."

Agnes shook her head. "I am a spring child, and I find no joy in it."

The Widow laughed brightly. "Well, perhaps you are not using your gift as you should. Tell me, what was your blessing?"

"I can move water from stream to house," Agnes said.

"Another lie," came the response. "Your gift is more powerful than that trifling thing, but no matter. That is not why you are here. Now, Agnes, I cannot summon a baby out of thin air. No cunning woman can do such a thing. You are aware of this, no?"

Agnes shook her head. She was not aware of anything, not really. Suddenly, the Widow Sewall leaned forward, lifting the bottom of the cup with her fingers, encouraging Agnes to drink all the liquid in one fell swoop. Agnes spluttered a little but obliged. Then, the Widow took the cup from her, staring into the empty vessel. She nodded.

"Yes. I thought it was you I had heard the rumours about. You embarrassed the family at the Spring Feast. I know more, perhaps, than you know. I have been visited by someone else who has your name on their lips. I rejected their offer, but they were perhaps successful."

Agnes frowned, her mouth tangy with the taste of the tea, savoury and sour. "What do you mean?"

"You are not with child for a reason, Agnes. A curse lays heavy on your name." The Widow sat back, widening her eyes matter-of-factly.

"How do you know?" Agnes asked.

"Because I am not the only cunning woman in the town, of course. There are others. And one in particular, who happens to be the mother-in-law of the man you attempted to...marry. Perhaps steal would be a better term?"

Agnes' skin flushed with embarrassment, and she felt the word 'steal' trickle across her pores.

"So, now you know. Everything has a price, Agnes. Children, marriage, wealth. All things cost. But I do not curse, no. What can you offer me, to help you?"

Agnes thought desperately. What could she offer? She had almost nothing, save for the clothes on her back, the skin on her face. "I have nothing, Widow Sewall."

The Widow observed her for a moment, nodding. "You think you have nothing, but if I help you, you shall offer something that was once promised to me. Unfortunately, the bearer of this promise now lies beneath the earth."

Agnes licked her dry lips, seeing the heat from the fire in the balmy spring air. She had no idea what the Widow was referring to.

"In a world such as ours, child, we face many risks. You yourself know all about risk, as does your family. Your brother left you to perish, he headed for the war, and your family could see the writing on the wall. You have a gift, but it is not the gift that I desire. If I help you, if I do this thing for you, then you must promise me that when the men of this town knock at my door, when they descend and try to drag me into the woods, you will speak up. You will say that I am not a witch, but rather a healer. For is it not so?" The Widow's eyes were plain and hard. Agnes found herself trying to see a softness in them, struggling to understand the request.

"Why would they do such a thing, Widow Sewall?" she asked, her voice hesitant and withdrawn. Within though, Agnes knew. Her feigned confusion was fooling neither of the women.

"There are rumours through the town that I am a witch, Agnes. A *witch*. I help women. I help women with birthing issues. I give them gifts the Gods cannot. The Grothi says that women like myself are to burn in hell, and I have been banned from his church. He has spread the word throughout the land that this is the case. And yet...do I believe him? The Gods speak to me in fits and bursts, but their voices are not clear."

Agnes frowned, lacing her fingers in and out of each other, curious and afraid. "But why have the men not come if this is the case?"

"They are afraid, Agnes. The women they drag into those woods know little of curses. Come, you know this, your own mother must have told you some things...they are afraid to knock on my door. And so, here I live, with the wood rotting about me, and not a person to replace the straw upon my roof."

"And so you wanted the cabbage because you cannot go to market...?" Agnes asked, the question sticking in her throat.

"Yes, yes, though I move at times. I visit others. When the cloud is heavy, and the streets are bare. And, of course, they cannot stop me from joining in the occasional festivity. Why, sometimes they are so set upon keeping their eyes peeled for a nefarious Widow that they miss me walk by." With an obvious biting of her cheek lining, the Widow topped up her tea.

Agnes cleared her throat, considering the offer. Clearly, she had not been the first to be asked, for what power did she hold in this town? There would be others, her voice would not be alone. And to be with child, that was the wish. That would solve all her problems, her lie, her family, old and new, and their feelings towards her.

"What do you say, Agnes?" Widow Sewall asked, taking a sip from her cup nonchalantly, as though she didn't care either way. Perhaps she didn't, Agnes mused. Maybe she had many women readied for just such an event.

"I...I say, I will," Agnes said, clearly. Her stomach ached with the words, as though it was an instantaneous thing. "Am I with child now?"

A small smile spread across the Widow Sewall's face, and she began to laugh. "With child already? Goodness me, Agnes, what a strange creature you are! What, do you think I am a God?"

Agnes placed her cup down on the floor beside her and breathed in sharply, the humiliation stinging. No, she did not think the Widow Sewall was a God. To think so was blasphemous. But to think that Agnes knew how this worked was an assumption too far.

"No." The Widow straightened her back, staring seriously at Agnes once more. "I cannot magic up a baby, as I said before. You must snip the hair of a woman with child, in order to gain what you desire."

Agnes nodded, thinking over the words. Of course, there were a few women in town who were pregnant, to whom she would have access. She thought of how she might do this, of what she would use to cut the hair. Some women wore it braided, piled upon their heads, and to reach for the strands would be to move too close to the skin. What would it mean to take a little of who they were and bring it to the Widow Sewall? It would mean safety, for herself, her family. A child, a reason to be loved. She would do it. There was one woman who wore her hair braided down her back, and sometimes down, as though a golden stream were caught in time. Agnes knew exactly who.

Chapter Sixteen

Silo had awoken in a jubilant mood, one that Agnes had never before witnessed. He sang as he dressed, making his way downstairs in his wedding outfit, and Agnes stared as he reached the kitchen, confused. As he laid eyes on her, he shook his head.

"Agnes, go, go change. It is Sunday!"

Agnes glanced down at her clothes, noting for the first time that day how stained her apron was, how her shoes were wearing through at the toe. She reached a hand to her hair and realised that she hadn't brushed it in days.

"Agnes," Silo said firmly, his gaze following hers. "You look a mess. Go and change for church. It will not do. We have news to deliver."

Nodding, Agnes took to the stairs, climbing two at a time. Of course, she realised, for Silo, today was special. She should have anticipated that he would be proud to deliver her to the front, beside the milk and honey bride who was also with child. It would give him reason to talk to his old friend Finn, reason to shake hands with the Grothi, without humiliation stinging his face. Staining his fate.

With great haste, Agnes pulled a comb through her hair, braiding it as best she could. She dressed in the now dusty wedding dress. She knew that she smelled, having not washed recently in the stream. What had happened, she wondered, since she washed last? She had told a lie. She had made a promise. And since that day, barely three sunrises ago, she had swept the floor of the kitchen and stuck her hands into the flames of the fire, knowing nothing but memories.

"Agnes! Will you hurry up? We shall be late." The words drifted up the stairs, and Agnes swallowed, feeling judgment rain down on her. She could hear Silo and Pa talking, murmurs that included her name. Without looking in the mirror, she pinched her cheeks and bit her lips, trying to make herself of milk and honey. On the way out the door, she pushed her small wedding knife into her pocket.

*

The church was busy, as usual, and the Grothi stood at the front, his hands by his side, palms up, waiting for silence to descend. Agnes took her place behind Saskia, standing at the front of the church with the other wives, head bowed.

"The Gods know that a town the size of ours cannot survive with more mouths to feed, and so they bless us with the loss at the same time as the giving. One has died since the marriage of our young wives, to be replaced by one babe in nine months. Daughters of the Gods, if you know that it is you of whom I speak, step forward."

His words were the same as the time before, the time before that, and the time before. Fear hitched in Agnes' throat as she realised that another woman might step forward. She bit her tongue and stepped, not knowing if anyone behind her moved also. The Grothi did not flinch and nodded at her, placing a hand on her shoulder.

"Bless you, our daughter, our wife, for you have already proven yourself to be one of us," he said, before staring at her a second too long, his eyes hard and bare. Agnes tried to smile. Did he know? Could he sense the lie, the untruth that she spouted through her movement?

"Ah," he began, glancing behind her. "For the Gods sometimes surprise us with another gift, a foretelling of a death to come. Here, child, for you also have proven yourself to be one of us." Agnes turned, making eye contact with another young bride, who blushed furiously as though it were she who was lying.

One by one, they were told to be seated again, and Agnes purposefully chose where she sat down. It was behind Saskia once more, whose hair was brushed and braided in a complicated pattern upon her head, stretching down her nape and back, beyond the wood of the church pew. Agnes breathed in. Honey wafted through her nostrils, as she knew it would. She would only have one chance, and it was when they closed their eyes in prayer. The Grothi droned on, talking of the war, of the people who protected them, of the world beyond their village. Agnes noticed the woman beside her try to shift away and felt momentarily self-conscious before remembering the truth of her reality.

"And as we bow our heads, we understand that the Gods have our future in their hands—"

The congregation breathed in collectively, bowing their heads. Agnes quickly glanced around, checking that everyone had their eyes closed, and reached for the knife. With care, she gently took the end of Saskia's complicated hair and sliced at the blonde cascade. Saskia didn't flinch, didn't even appear to notice, so deep were her prayers. Once both the hair and the knife had been pocketed, Agnes closed her eyes, whispering the words in time with the Grothi. The hair felt heavy, alive, waiting beside her.

"Praise be to the Gods, who selected us for mercy. May we do our best and visit them weekly. May we pay our tithes for their benefit. May our children be blessed with the gifts of spring."

Agnes opened her eyes, glancing around. The congregation began to move, her pew emptying quicker than others. Silo stood at the end of the aisle, a small smile on his face. He noticed that Finn stood just behind him, and the two turned and spoke for a moment, shaking hands heartily.

"Come, Wife," Silo said when she neared, "for Sunday is a day of rest, and the meat will not cook itself."

Finn sniggered, and Agnes heard a breathy laugh coming from behind her, the scent of honey soaring with it. They laughed because they did have someone to cook the meat for them, Agnes knew. They laughed because they weren't her. They laughed because Saskia was truly with child.

Chapter Seventeen

The hair was waiting. Agnes had tried to take it to the Widow Sewall three times without luck. Each time, Silo had woken, shifting from his sleep and asking Agnes where she was going. Since the service, it was as though he slept on a spike, waking often and checking on her and, she imagined, the baby.

On the fourth night, Agnes fed Silo extra. She had planned it, saving up some scraps from the days before, building the fire higher than ever in the grate. When the time came for rest, she did the unthinkable: Agnes initiated the crawl across the bed, laid her hand on his shoulder. He did not refuse. Her efforts worked. When she climbed out of bed on Thursday night, Silo did not stir.

*

The journey to the Widow Sewall's house was easier than before, now that Agnes knew the way. She crept through the darkness, watching the moon above her, and wondered about the Gods. Were they watching as she walked through the town, and did they know where she was going? Perhaps they watched her waste her blessing at her mother's request and were punishing her for it, her hidden blessing the reason that she was not with child, that her skin was not touched by a man like Finn and instead stank like urine.

The Widow Sewall waited at the door, the fire bright behind her, the silhouette of her body visible from yards away. As she drew closer, the Widow nodded, stepping aside and letting Agnes in.

"You have arrived. It has taken you some time, no? I expected you sooner."

"My husband kept waking as I tried to leave," Agnes explained, suddenly tired and aware that she hadn't slept properly all week.

The Widow Sewall observed Agnes closely as she closed the door, shaking her head as though disappointed. "He is suspicious, most likely. And yet, you are here. Did you claim what I asked you for?"

Agnes reached into her pocket and pulled out the golden hairs, placing them into the Widow's outstretched palm. She barely looked at the hair, just carried it over to the pot that bubbled above the fire and took what seemed like an endlessly long sigh.

"Into the fire she goes," Widow Sewall murmured, tossing the hair into the dark liquid. She waited a moment, muttering under her breath, and then nodded.

"Come, Agnes, come here." From her pocket, the Widow pulled out a small silver spoon, handing it over. Agnes took it, noting the delicacy of the engraving. Indeed, she had never seen anything so fine. It was probably worth more than her house. And to think, this was how the woman was living, destitute but with such riches around her.

"You must repeat after me and then sip the liquid. Do you understand?"

Agnes nodded, waiting, still fascinated by the spoon.

"I look to take what is not mine. I am worthy of a child."

Agnes repeated the words, feeling the word worthy stick slightly on her tongue. Was she worthy? There was nothing for it now. She dipped the spoon into the liquid and noticed, with a grimace, that a hair was stretched out towards her mouth.

"Sip," the Widow directed, and Agnes pushed all thoughts from her mind and sipped, tasting the sharp and bitter broth, feeling it slip down her throat. Once done, the Widow snatched the spoon from Agnes' hand and stared at her.

"It should be done by the time you wake up tomorrow. The curse that was on your head was not so powerful that it could not be undone. Remember, it is your job to look after the child. You are its mother. And when they come for me, you must speak up."

*

During the weeks that passed, Agnes barely slept, feeling the weight of her decisions heavy on the bed, as the taste of their daily broth turned to bile. She was with child, she knew, her body telling her in hints and whispers.

This particular morning was the worst yet. She lay, watching the darkness change to light, knowing that she ought to get up and start breakfast. And yet, her body was heavy, laden with aches, and nausea began to seep through to her consciousness.

She watched as Silo climbed out of bed, starting when he saw that she was still lying beside him.

"What are you doing, Wife? The breakfast must be cooked before Pa and I are downstairs. Why do you lie so?"

Agnes winced at the accusation. He was correct; she was a liar. He had outed her secret. She thought of all the things she could say that might explain why she had done what she had done, the expectations that weighed on her head, the way he looked at her with such hatred.

"Wife. Agnes. Why do you lie here this way? Are you unwell?"

She breathed out slowly. He was not accusing her, not yet. He was asking after her health.

"I am unwell," Agnes said slowly. "I feel sick and tired, as though covered in weights."

"Well, yes, it is pregnancy. My stepmother went through the same. I had wondered why you were keeping so well, and it seems the child has finally caught up with you. And yet, Saskia goes about her day with the same feelings, Finn tells me, and doesn't miss any of her chores." Silo finished this last sentence poignantly, his eyebrows raising as he spoke.

"Saskia," Agnes said, as she pulled herself up and tried not to vomit, "has maids."

Silo's face hardened, and he shook his head firmly.

"Today, Agnes. You have one day. Visit your mother or one of the local Widows for some type of remedy to your sickness. If you are the same tomorrow, I will know that you have not done so, and we will have to visit the Grothi."

With that, Silo stalked out of the room and thundered down the stairs. After a moment, Agnes could hear quiet discussions, her name drifting up the wooden staircase, and tuts.

The phrase, "You're too good to her, boy," floated around the room. Agnes retched, swallowing back down sick. She listened to the door open and close. They were too good to her.

"Agnes."

The voice she had not heard in a time filtered through the walls again now, soft and quiet but unmistakably there.

"Agnes."

Agnes lay back down, her body throbbing. "What do you want?" she responded.

"Agnes. I know…"

COLERIC SUMMER

Chapter Eighteen

Her mother was her first appointment. She welcomed Agnes with open arms, made tea, and settled her in front of the fire, although the day was warm.

"Child, you are ever so pale. What ails you?"

Agnes sighed, the sickness coming again as it had the entire walk over. She knew she was pale, felt sweat pop from her pores, and shivered despite feeling no chill or breeze upon her flesh. The heat was nothing she was familiar with. This was coming from within, from deeper inside her skin. "I am not myself, Mother. The pregnancy is making me…"

Another rush of bile, as though the baby was playing with her weasand. Her mother frowned gently, placing a hand on her forehead. It reminded Agnes of when she was small and occasionally unwell, and how her mother used to comfort her, her hands always smooth and fresh, despite the weather.

"It is odd, but I never felt such a thing when I was with child. Neither did your grandmother."

Agnes sipped her drink and nodded, instinctively knowing the reason. Whatever the Widow Sewall had done had worked, of course, but it had its consequences.

"Oh. So, you cannot help with any cures?" Agnes asked, her father walking through the door.

"Cures? For what?"

"For the sickness, the child is making her sick," her mother answered, shrugging.

"Oh, you will want to visit Saskia, then. Or perhaps her mother," her father answered, patting Agnes gently on the head. She felt so small again, young, as though she could stay forever, curled up in what was still her home. "She has had such terrible sickness; she may be able to help."

The meaning of this was clearly lost on her parents, for they had no idea what she had done. But to Agnes, it was quite clear. There was a reason she felt so terrible, and there was a reason it didn't run in the family.

*

Agnes agreed to her mother's rare invitation for a walk to the butchers, her mother grabbing her by the arm. For the first time, she seemed proud of her daughter. Agnes yawned as they walked, and instead of tapping her on the hand and telling her to act accordingly, she smiled wanly at passers-by.

"She's with child, poor thing, hardest part is the first few months."

Murmurs of agreement fell back to the pair, and Agnes raised her chin, proud, until they reached the butchers. The stench was overpowering. The metallic fresh scent of blood battled with the smell of stale sawdust, the fresh sprigs of sage and rosemary which hung outside the shop doing nothing to battle the scent of animals slaughtered on site. Agnes buried her nose in her apron, longing for her tannery's familiar odour. Her mother glanced at her, smiling slowly.

"Ah, of course. Wait here, child, I'll be but a moment."

She waited while her mother went into the butchers, holding her breath as often as possible, sucking in sections of air as quickly as she could. As she waited, glimmers of conversation reached her ears.

"Well, she is with child, I thought treat—"

Agnes smiled. Her mother was buying her a treat. Silo would be pleased. Perhaps he would forgive her for her laziness that day.

"Ginger? Ah yes, I shall tell her."

More murmurs. The voice of the butcher's wife filtered in, though her pitch was too high to hear. Mumbles. Then, her mother's response.

"Is that so? I am sorry to hear it. Of course, I can pass by."

Agnes strained to listen, and then, her mother appeared beside her, giving a tight smile.

"Right, come now, Agnes. I have a piece of mutton for you, a small treat to help you feel better. They say that ginger helps your sickness. But, before we make our way, we must visit Saskia's home. It's bad news, I'm afraid, and the butcher's wife has a piece of beef to give her. I have said that we will drop it off to help the poor girl."

Agnes nodded, knowing without asking: Saskia had lost her baby—the same one Agnes had gained. Bile rose in her throat, tasting faintly of honey.

Chapter Nineteen

The maid answered the door with a curtsey, and Agnes' mother bustled over, taking over the situation as soon as she saw the dimness of the corridor. The maid nodded, taking the package.

"Your gift is much appreciated, ma'am, but the mistress won't be up for seeing you."

"I don't expect her to be, but if we could have a moment with her husband, it would be appreciated," her mother said, brushing over the fact that she had merely passed over the meat, it being a gift from the butcher, and not herself. The maid nodded, showing them into the front room, where Agnes had been before. They sat awkwardly, and Agnes watched the bright flowers outside the window, which seemed to wilt in their presence.

"Mother, we didn't need to come in–" Agnes began, rolling her eyes as her mother lifted a finger to her lips. Agnes could only think one thing: would the men be coming to take Saskia to the woods?

"Mother, do you think the men will–"

Her mother glared at her, shaking her head once. "No, Agnes. Not this family, no. Now shush, lest they hear you."

After a moment, the door opened, and Finn stood inside the frame. The handsome sparkle that Agnes had become used to seeing in his smile was gone, replaced by small, thin lips. Bags beneath his eyes told of his lack of sleep the night before, and as he stepped in, Agnes smelled not honey, but sweat.

"Good afternoon," he said, his eyes dull.

Agnes opened her mouth to speak but was silenced by her mother's voice. "We are so sorry for your loss. We wanted to say that if there is anything we can do for your family, you must let us know. We have given a piece of beef to your maid in the hopes that it will give your dear wife strength."

Finn nodded, offering the briefest of smiles before it disappeared again, a flash of lightning in a dark storm. "You are kind, I thank you. And you, Agnes, are you well?" His eyes flickered to her stomach, and as they did so, Agnes felt a surge of acid bubble up from her throat and hit the back of her tongue.

"I am, thank you. My husband sends his good wishes, also."

Finn acknowledged this with straight lips and raised eyebrows. "Thank you. If that's all, I must be getting back to my work."

"Of course," the women said in unison, dipping their heads as they spoke. Finn disappeared upstairs, and the maid came to collect them from the room. As they walked past the steps, Agnes heard Saskia up above. The words were clear.

"Is she still with child?"

"She is."

A sob. Agnes' stomach fluttered at the sound of its mother's voice.

*

"Terrible news," Silo said, ripping another piece of bread from the loaf. Agnes watched as he dipped it in the sheep's succulent juices, observing that he nodded slightly while chewing, a sign she now knew was an indication that he was enjoying his food.

"Hmm. It is awful news," Pa responded. "You saw the girl, Saskia?" His watery eyes reached Agnes in the dim candlelight of evening, and she shook her head.

"No, I did not."

"Well, the Grothi was quite clear that the numbers did not match. He said it himself. The Gods have spared a life from the village," Pa said, pushing a piece of meat into his mouth and chewing avidly.

Agnes quailed. It was true, when she had stepped forward, there had been another woman there standing beside her, and the

Grothi had said there should be only one. For some strange reason, her mind flickered to her brother, and she wondered what he was doing right at that moment.

"The war comes closer, the cobbler told me today," Silo said, changing the subject. Agnes glanced up at him, wondering if he could read her mind. "The war comes ever closer," he said again, hammering home the point.

"The war is a fool's game. The kingdom is just," said Pa, closing down the conversation. They sat in silence for a moment, and Agnes breathed in audibly, causing both men to look at her.

"My father will have a delivery man collect his swords on Friday, and then we shall have more news."

"Hmmm," Pa said, shaking his head. "The kingdom is just. Your brother was a fool."

Silence descended upon the table, and Agnes felt her eyes begin to sting. She had not mentioned her brother.

"But you are to make up for his shortcomings, Wife," Silo added, patting her hand without a smile. "And we are to thank for bringing your family back to the glory of the Gods."

Agnes nodded, eyes fixed on her plate, gritting her teeth in silence.

"Agnes."

She glanced up, staring at the two men. "Yes?"

They looked at each other, and Silo shook his head. "We neither of us spoke, Wife. Is there any more meat?"

Chapter Twenty

Friday came fast, and Agnes had pushed herself to wake up before the cockerel once more, sweeping the hearth and vomiting in a bucket beneath the table at her stilted leisure. Her only intention that day was to make it to her father to help with the loading of the swords. Silo would have banned it had he known, but Agnes knew that a new shipment of skins would arrive at the weekend, and they were preparing for it, making space and folding up pieces of leather, hustling to sell what they could to the cobbler.

She felt desperate to go, but even as she asked herself why, she couldn't quite articulate it. What did she hope for? In some ways, it was that her brother would be driving the wagon from the capital, as though that was at all realistic. In others, that the driver might have very specific news, that he could tell her of how the war was going, perhaps even of having seen a young man who looked much like her. Her heart was lying to her, she knew, and yet to stay away would be the hardest thing yet.

Once the men had left the house, Agnes dressed carefully. Her stomach was starting to round softly beneath her, showing the signs of early pregnancy, and to look at it made her feel strange, nauseated in a new way. When would the baby start kicking? She didn't know. All she knew was that the creature within felt as though it was forcing its way out as if it knew she wasn't its real mother. She paused at the door as another wave of sickness threatened to rise to her mouth. There was no time for this, she admonished herself. She had things to do.

*

She arrived at her parents' as the sun had settled in the sky and saw her father preparing the swords outside. He glanced up, acknowledging her presence with a nod.

"Agnes, today is not the day for chat and oats. I have to prepare this shipment for the kingdom. The man will be here any moment." His eyes glanced over her new shape, pausing on the belly that showed beneath her apron.

"Yes, Father, I am aware. In truth, I came to help."

Her father chuckled, rolling his eyes and turning back to his swords. "You are with child. You cannot help an old blacksmith in his work."

Agnes stepped forward, determined to show different, and bent down to select a piece of leather to wrap one of the edges of steel. Her father gave her a sharp tap on the hand.

"Take heed, child, I told you no."

Agnes paused and rose up again, swallowing.

"Father...what if it is...someone we know driving the cart?"

Her father frowned, then looked into the distance.

"Here he comes now. Someone we know? Well, it will be; the kingdom's carrier has been the same the last three years."

"Oh. Where is your apprentice?"

"Agnes, I am busy. He is busy sourcing ore at the mine. What is it that you want?" Her father stared at her, his eyes hard and unflinching.

"I thought the carrier might have news of my brother."

There was a silence that trickled through the air before them, strong and loud in its lack of noise.

"He has no news of your brother. None of them do, and no news will tell us anything beyond what we already know. Do stop bothering me, Agnes. A tanner's wife must be fairly busy. Do you have nothing to do?"

Agnes breathed in, smelling the freshness of the air around her family home, and tried a smile. "I could be helpful to you, Father, if you remember my gift. That gift has no place in a tanner's home, and yet in a blacksmith's—"

"Enough. Go home, Agnes. Tend the hearth, cook the food. Prepare for your upcoming birth. I do not need a pregnant daughter struggling to lift swords for me."

With this, he turned his back, and Agnes nodded. She began to walk away, slowly, in the same direction the cart from the kingdom was taking. It rumbled ever closer. Agnes quickened her step.

As the driver neared, he raised a hand. Agnes responded, turning back quickly to see if her father had noticed. He had gone inside, no doubt, to fetch the invoice.

"Good morning, sir!" Agnes shouted, watching as the cart slowed. It came to a stop beside her, and the young man gave a toothy grin, his skin flushed from the journey. His eyes crinkled in a kindness that Agnes hadn't seen in a long time.

"Good morning, ma'am. You are the blacksmith's daughter, are you not? I recognise you from years ago." His accent lilted up at the end in the way those from the kingdom did. Agnes smiled gently, dipping her head.

"I am. Tell me, what news of the kingdom?"

The man scratched his chin and shrugged. "The war continues. Our leaders are just and fair and give us everything we need."

Agnes nodded, a placatory smile on her lips. "I thank the Gods daily for their care and love. Tell me, any news of the rebels?"

The delivery man recoiled at the mention of the word, frowning. He glanced around him, as though they were flanked by people, and then leaned forward. "For what reason will you know of the rebels, girl? You are clearly with child, you cannot expect to join them? And they do not take so kindly to women. It is a dangerous thing, asking after the enemy."

Agnes forced a laugh out of her mouth, the noise tinny and strange. "To join them? I have never left my home here. Why, the people of Locklear stay in Locklear. No, no, I am happy with my place in life. Although, I ask because my brother joined and I—"

"Ah. Your brother joined, did he? Well, with the best will in the world, girl, he has most likely met his end. The Gods do us well in their care of the kingdom, and if you were there…you would see the heads of all the rebels that have been caught to date lined up on spikes outside the castle walls. You would see the burning of their weapons. The rebels are losing fast, and your brother will not have been successful in his attempts. Strange, I have worked with your father for a few years now, and he has never mentioned a son to me."

His gaze fell forward, and Agnes turned to see her father waiting outside the homestead, far off in the distance. Sickness washed over her body again, and she knew, almost instantly, that she had made a grave error. The man shook his head and then clicked his tongue, driving his horse onwards. Agnes watched him leave, saw her father wave his hand, and stood, watching their transaction for a moment. She collected her skirts and turned back to the village, knowing that she would receive a visit from her parents before too long.

Chapter Twenty-One

"And so, we welcome a gift at this time of year, the generous Widow Pluck, who has travelled from beyond the Principality of Hargothrest to be with us today. Widow Pluck, I speak on behalf of the mothers here today when I say, thank you for visiting us." The Grothi bowed deeply, his eyes resting on the ground in front of the grandly dressed Widow Pluck. Agnes knew her face from the years before. Her cream, creaseless outfit had always given the impression of otherworldliness. Agnes breathed in, trying to keep her sickness down, sitting among the other wives. The church was filled to the brim, the usual scenario for the Widow's arrival.

"While I am here, the Grothi and I have decided that any woman who is with child may also come to me to discuss their health. As you know, I am primarily here for the babies of spring, to deliver their blessings alongside your most esteemed Grothi, but I shall hold office hours here for a while." The Widow bowed her head to the crowd of onlookers, her cream bonnet puckering at the seams. Agnes hesitated to glance about her.

Saskia was sitting in the same row at the end. Agnes ran her eyes over her pale skin, her downward gaze, her sunken cheeks. Her hair, usually so beautifully braided and kept, was unbrushed, tied back with a piece of string. She looked tired, or perhaps beyond so, worn down, as if she hadn't slept in years. Agnes' heart began to thud in her ears. She wanted to reach out, to say something, to apologise. But what was there to say? As if sensing that she was being watched, Saskia's gaze drifted over to Agnes. They caught eyes. Despite herself, Agnes mouthed the words, "I'm sorry." Saskia nodded, allowing the offer of apology, and let her stare rest upon Agnes' stomach. She couldn't know, Agnes told herself. There was no possible way she could know what had happened, and even if she did, could she blame her? The world had taken against Agnes from the moment she was given the wrong blessing, from the second her brother was taken by the promise of adventure, and her family's future had rested on her shoulders.

Agnes turned her attention back to the front of the church where the Widow Pluck was saying a prayer. In keeping with the rest of the room, she, too, bowed her head and closed her eyes. Of course, Saskia would blame her if she told her the truth, if she mentioned her visit to the Widow Sewall. But Saskia was graced with luck, with possibilities that Agnes could never have. And if Agnes really tried, really thought about it very carefully...she believed that Saskia would do the same thing to her.

*

"You must wait to see the Widow Pluck, Wife, and come back to the homestead afterwards. I shall do you this kindness and begin the dinner." Silo's gaze hardened slightly as he leaned into Agnes' ear and lowered his voice. "A one-time kindness," he whispered, his breath pungent on her skin. Agnes nodded.

A short queue had already formed. Some women were late with child and expecting their babies soon, and others freshly pregnant, suspecting so, or, like Saskia, heavy with disappointment. Agnes stood behind her in the queue, still catching a whisper of honey as she moved. It was mixed with something else now, something that held more weight. Agnes found it hard to put into words, but she knew it when she smelled it. It was the same scent her mother had given off when her brother had disappeared. It was sorrow.

"Agnes," Saskia said, nodding her head.

"Saskia. Are you well?" Agnes asked, immediately regretting the question. She was not, it was clear.

Saskia shrugged her shoulders, glancing up at Agnes' eyes. She shook her head and then sighed. "There will be another chance, I am sure. I am here to ask the Widow Pluck if she has any experience of...what has happened with me."

Agnes nodded, folding her arms in front of her stomach as though it might change what Saskia knew about her. "I am sure that she will be able to help. Of course, your position is not so unusual...you shall be with child once more."

Saskia glanced around her as though ready to divulge a secret and then leaned in. "Agnes, you don't understand. It's not... normal."

Agnes' heart thudded in her ears again and she breathed in sharply. Did she know? Was she about to say something? "Go on..."

"My mother lost a child before she had me, and I know what to look out for. There should be...signs. But, Agnes, I went to bed with child. I was starting to show, I had the sickness, but it didn't trouble me. But then...I woke up, and I was no longer with child. I felt it as soon as I woke. It wasn't as though I had lost the baby, Agnes. There just was no baby. I knew it."

Agnes glanced around them, seeing a few of the women in the queue listening in. They exchanged glances, and Agnes squirmed under their watch, placing a hand on Saskia's arm. "I am sorry to hear it, Saskia. You have the support of the town, and I don't doubt that you will soon be with child again," she repeated. It was all she could think to do, repeat the old promise which she had no authority to fulfil. Agnes also knew that Saskia did have the support of the town. As her mother had confirmed, one did not take a member of such a high-born family to the woods for such an experience. That was saved for troublesome, lower-born women.

"Agnes," Saskia's eyes grew wider, and her voice fell to a deeper and quieter tone. She looked desperate, pleading, her hand gripping Agnes' own. "The Widow Tideswell said it isn't the first time that this has happened. She said someone must have taken the baby."

The women around them gasped, and Agnes took a step back before realising that it hadn't been by choice. She looked down, seeing the Grothi's hand on her arm. He smiled a faux, benevolent smile and nodded at Saskia.

"Child, the Widow Pluck will see you now. Come, you can skip the queue. I am sure none of these generous wives will mind." Agnes bowed her head in deference to his lordship, but not before she saw the look in Saskia's eyes. She was afraid.

Chapter Twenty-Two

By the time Agnes' turn came, the sun had almost dipped out of the sky. The church was getting dark and dour, and some of the women before and behind her in the queue had left already, saying they would be back the next day. Agnes couldn't return, she knew. Silo's kindness was an occasional thing, and that meant that this was her only opportunity to speak to the Widow Pluck. She hadn't seen Saskia leave the room, but she must have. There must have been another door inside, and perhaps her mother had collected her, hurrying her home to Finn under cloaks and love.

Eventually, the large wooden door opened, and the Widow Pluck stood silhouetted by candlelight. Her cream gown was now creased, and she beckoned to Agnes.

"Come, child, you have waited long."

Agnes bowed her head and entered the room, empty but for two stools and a long wooden table with a book upon it. Agnes sat on one of the stools and, before the Widow could speak, began.

"Is Saskia well?"

"Saskia?" The Widow frowned, then checked the book on the table, running a finger down the page. "Ah. You are a friend of hers?" She pulled up the other stool and sat down noiselessly. Her face was wrinkled, showing her age, and yet there was youth in her eyes. They were so clear that it was like looking through a stream.

"Yes," Agnes responded, knowing that the single word was an exaggeration.

"Hmm." The Widow briefly reviewed the book again and sighed. "She is in mourning. I could not say that any two women mourn the same, and we should not expect them to. For now, be a friend, listen to her words, but do not put too much credence in them."

Agnes hesitated, and then breathed out the sentence she had been afraid to say, all at once, "She said that the Widow Tideswell told her that someone took her baby."

The Widow gave a sad smile and nodded. "Yes, this is something that she repeated to me also. I have worked with the Widow Tideswell, and she is an accomplished birth hand, for those who can afford her. I would not think that she said something so drastic, so for now, put it out of your mind."

Agnes nodded. In many ways, that was exactly what she had wanted to hear, and yet it was a heart-wrenching thought. Saskia wasn't lying, and Agnes knew it. Perhaps the Widow Pluck did, too.

"So, you are with child."

"I am, Widow Pluck," Agnes responded, "Though how far along I do not know."

"Hmm. I see you are already showing a little. Any issues?"

"Sickness."

"Yes. You are pale. And your husband is a tanner, which cannot help. It is things that we surround ourselves with that have an impact on our pregnancy. You are a child of the spring, are you not?"

Agnes nodded, trying a smile. Now that she was used to the scent of the tannery, it surprised her that other people could still smell it. But of course, she realised, she must smell as bad as Silo had when she first met him.

"Hmm. And you use your gift for the good of your community?" the Widow asked, her gaze unflinching. Agnes let the room fill with silence, unsure what to say.

"You do not, then," the Widow filled in the space, matter-of-factly. Agnes studied her face. Could she know what it was that Agnes had been gifted with?

"I...um...I do use it to help my husband and his father, yes," Agnes bleated.

The Widow seemed now preoccupied, writing something down in her book. "A small use for a large gift," she said.

"You know what my spring blessing was, Widow Pluck? Are not they divined from the Gods?"

The Widow's head snapped up, and she shook it with a cold glare. "Of course they are. Your Grothi and I are simply a channel, and trust me, even if I were party to your or anyone else's gift, there are too many to remember."

Once again, silence began to diminish the space between the women. Agnes felt small in the Widow's presence, unsure, as though she had been caught out for something. What that was, she couldn't say. The Widow stood then, indicating that she was to touch Agnes' stomach. Agnes nodded, moving her hands to her side awkwardly, waiting. With firm fingers, the Widow prodded and poked her slightly swollen belly, murmuring under her breath. After a minute of this, she paused, and then stared at Agnes, her eyes wide. Agnes' heartbeat grew loud once more, sickness threatening to rise in her throat.

"What is it, Widow Pluck? Is the baby well?"

The Widow stepped back, hands still outstretched, and nodded. "Yes. Yes, the child is...the child is fine. Up now, the next woman will be waiting. Take ginger for your sickness. Up now, up now." The Widow wafted her hands around Agnes as though she were a fly and stepped towards the door. Agnes stood quickly, following the Widow. As she reached her aged hand out to the door handle, she turned to Agnes and cocked her head.

"You are aware, perhaps, that it is not your time?" she asked. Agnes swallowed spit and shook her head. Another lie.

"In whichever case...the child is fine. The child is fine," the Widow repeated. "The mother is...you will make do. Leave now. If you have any further questions, and you can afford her, take them to the Widow Tideswell. If you do not have the coin," she opened the door, and stared through Agnes, as if she could see right into her soul, "the Widow Sewall."

She knew. Agnes lifted her chin, tears threatening to burst from her eyes, and gave a slight curtsey. The Widow knew, but she wasn't going to say anything. How could she prove it, anyway? A strange confidence washed through Agnes for the first time since all of this began. She remembered the Widow Sewall's words. It was her child now, and no one could prove otherwise.

Chapter Twenty-Three

The oats were burned the next morning. Agnes doled them out into the bowls as usual, placing them in front of Silo and Pa. The latter had come into the kitchen quietly, as Agnes had been moving the logs through the flames, driving them upwards. How long he had been behind her, she could not be sure, but when he cleared his throat, she had pulled her hands back from the fire, standing quickly to smooth down her apron. Now, he sat looking at the bowl, the darkened oats before him, a slight frown on his face.

"Finn told me the news yesterday," Silo said, picking up a spoon and digging it into his bowl. He pushed a spoonful of the food into his mouth and winced. "It's burned. Why is my breakfast burned?"

Agnes dipped her head, a glimmer of faux sorrow. "My apologies, Husband. I felt a wave of sickness as I cooked, and it stopped me from attending to the oats as I should. But please, do go on with your news." Pa glanced at Agnes and then back at his food, not moving.

"I don't want this to happen again, Agnes. This is the only food we have in the morning, and Pa and I have to work a full day on this. The Widow Pluck and your mother were supposed to help you with your sickness, did they not? Should I organise a meeting with the Grothi?"

Agnes sniffed, the tang of the air suddenly registering as it used to. "No, Silo, but thank you. A meeting with the Grothi will not be needed. I shall go out today and fetch some ginger, which should help the sickness."

"Speak of your news, boy," Pa said stiffly.

"Finn has been building a new house. Stone. It's being delivered from beyond the river."

Silence. Agnes shivered despite noticing the heat in the air from the hearth and the heavy summer sun bearing down on the wooden house. Stone. She watched Silo as he plunged his spoon into his bowl once more, knowing what that meant to him. The cost of couriering stone from another town was so beyond their reach. Agnes opened her mouth to speak but found herself bleating into nothing, distracted by a banging on the door.

"Agnes!"

Her father's voice. Agnes' face flushed at the sound, so strange was it to hear him here. He had never visited, not since she married. She hesitated, feeling a panic rise in her chest. Was there something wrong, some sort of emergency? Silo had placed his spoon down and was standing, making his way to the door. Agnes took this as a cue to remain seated, watching and waiting.

"Agnes!" came the shout again. Silo pulled open the door, and there, as expected, stood her father.

"Silo. May I have a word with your wife?" Her father's voice was clipped and stilted, and he waited until Silo nodded before turning to face his daughter. "Agnes, outside. Now."

Silo turned to Agnes with a slight frown, clearly curious as to what she had done to warrant such a tone. Agnes moved to respond to the urgency of his voice.

"Father," Agnes said, standing. She slipped out of the door into the morning sun. It was already beating down upon them, and Agnes squinted in the bright light, turning to her father. His face was drawn and thin, his eyes tired. "Has something happened to Mother?"

"No. Something has happened to my *livelihood*, Agnes. My *living*. What did you say to the delivery man from the kingdom? What did you say?"

Agnes stepped back from her father, shifting her weight in her boots. She had never seen him so angry before, his fists clenching and unclenching, his jaw ajar and stiff. Agnes shook her head.

"What do you mean? I don't understand," she breathed, trying to get him to lower his tone.

"You—" He shook himself as though trying to refocus on the words. "We received a letter from the kingdom. They have cancelled all future orders and will be using a blacksmith from elsewhere. They stated," her father's voice lowered dramatically, and he leaned in, baring his teeth once more, "that it was because of our family's allegiance to the war. How could that be, Agnes? I have never mentioned it. Your mother has never mentioned it. As far as we are concerned, we no longer have a son. All we have is a silly girl with another silly girl within her."

Agnes pulled her hand to her stomach and shook her head. "It could be a boy," she said plainly, "and—"

"Ha! A boy? With our luck, it'll be a girl. You said something to that man, and I watched you stop him. Did you mention your brother?"

Agnes pulled her mind back to the conversation she had had with the delivery man. Of course, she had mentioned her brother, she knew that. That was the whole reason she had gone.

"I asked after him," she admitted, stepping back to contend with the poor reaction that would surely come her way. Her father simply shook his head, his shoulders dropping.

"I knew it. You are as silly a child as ever. I don't know what else we can do, Agnes. You try and foil us at every turn—"

"This is not true. I am with child, Father." She placed both hands on each side of her stomach as though proving her efforts, her point.

Her father's eyes glanced down and then back up to her. "I shall pray that the Grothi does not hear about your error. I shall pray that we somehow find someone in this town who needs us for more than the occasional horseshoe. I shall pray that one day you will know what it is to hold your family's livelihood in your hands." With this, her father turned and stalked away. Agnes' stomach fluttered beneath her fingers, and with a retch, she leaned forward and expelled burned porridge onto the dirt floor.

Behind her, the door swung open. "Pour some water over that, Wife. And be quick about it. The stench is too much to bear," Silo uttered, pushing past her.

Agnes glanced up, wiping the sick residue from her mouth, and caught eyes with Pa. He blinked purposefully, as if taking her face in for the first time. Then he followed his son, away from the house. Perhaps he had seen more than she hoped.

Chapter Twenty-Four

After the water had washed away her vomit, days passed and gathered into a week, barely acknowledged. Agnes' nausea remained, though she breathed not a word to Silo. She sat before the fire, letting it die down in the hearth. Her legs were strange beneath her, wobbly, unsure, and she closed her eyes, just for a moment.

"Agnes."

Her eyes snapped open. That voice, again. She raised her hand to her forehead and shifted on the wooden seat. A headache was starting to set in, thumping its way through her skull. She opened her mouth to speak, to respond, but found that her voice was stifled by a sound at the door—a knocking. Surely, it would be her mother, coming to apologise, to beg for her to rejoin their family. With a juddering footstep, Agnes made her way to the door. As she reached it, it swung open, and there stood someone she had only ever seen by candlelight. It was the Widow Sewall.

Agnes stepped back at the sight of her, so unexpected. Her dark cloak billowed around her, and she reached up her hand and pulled her hood down, manoeuvring the basket in her arms to one side.

"May I come in?" she asked, her voice quiet yet strong. Agnes nodded, glancing behind the old woman, hoping that Silo and Pa had not seen her come onto the land. The Widow busily pushed past Agnes and sat down beside the table, placing her basket upon it. With care, she pulled out a large piece of ginger and put it on the table. Agnes closed the door behind her and hesitated, before sitting opposite.

"Ah, ginger. Thank you, Widow Sewall, for your kindness, I have been suffering—"

"With sickness, yes. How might I know that, Agnes?"

Agnes cleared her throat. "It is a common ailment."

"Hmm. You are aware, perhaps, that Saskia is having a new house built? Her husband has graciously provided everything needed to help her feel comfortable in her home. It is to be built of stone."

Agnes nodded, unsure why the Widow Sewall would come to tell her this. It was newsworthy, yes, but had little to do with her.

"Saskia is with child."

There was a pause. Agnes baulked at the news, shaking her head. "I am with child."

"You are. And so is Saskia. I had a visit from a woman I am not so friendly with, the Widow Pluck. You visited her, did you not? Along with Saskia?"

Agnes felt the child flutter beneath her skin, and nodded once more, her mouth suddenly dry.

"Yes. You did. A strange move, as you must know that the Widow Pluck is a powerful birth hand, almost as powerful as myself. Why you would not come to see me about your sickness, I do not know. For now, the Widow Pluck is fully aware of what you have done."

Agnes felt that honeyed bile rise anew in her throat, and stared across at the old woman, whose face was so stern that it almost resembled stone. She rolled her shoulders back, trying to regain a piece of that confidence she had felt when she looked into the Widow Pluck's eyes.

"What *we* have done, Widow Sewall," she responded. The woman smiled at this as though it were a great joke. She paused, looking about her at the kitchen, at the table, at the hearth, and eventually, raised her gaze to the rafters.

"Do you feel a heaviness in this house, Agnes?" she asked, her eyes still resting on the ceiling.

Agnes frowned. "Do you mean the scent? You get used to it."

"No, not that. Although how you get used to it, I don't know.

It's like stepping into an alley of cat's piss. No, it's something else. Do you know what happened to your mother-in-law?"

Agnes felt a weight rest on her shoulders, as though hands were pushing her down into the wooden stool she sat upon. She thought of Silo and Pa, living with another woman, and the things that they had told Agnes of that time. It was almost nothing.

"Well, she…she died," Agnes whispered, feeling the words creep out of her mouth like a secret.

The Widow Sewall cocked her head to one side, her eyes sharp, but with a hint of kindness.

"She did die. I knew her well. Your mother-in-law wasn't the mild-mannered woman you may think of when you imagine a tanner's wife. Well, for a start, she was a spring child. You, of course, know all about this. She had a power bestowed on her that was perhaps the most powerful gift any child had been given. She could bind the mouth of any sinner. And here's the trick, Agnes. We are all sinners. So, to have a friend like that, well, it was both a blessing and a curse."

Agnes shifted in her seat again and shook her head. "Why are you telling me this?"

"Because she bound the mouth of her husband, your father-in-law, when he found out that she was with a child that wasn't her own. Silo wasn't her child, you know, and she was your father-in-law's second wife after Silo's mother died. She was desperate for a child and came to me in much the same state you did. What perfection, I thought, to have this strong woman on side, who can bind the mouth of anyone who threatens to out me as a witch. But no, Agnes, for your father-in-law found out. Suspecting something was wrong, he followed her to one of our appointments one night. Let us cut a long tale short. Your father-in-law said she was a witch, and that he would tell the Grothi. These people are afraid of the Grothi, as though he is a God himself. Your mother-in-law bound his tongue, as far as I know. The next day, she was found hanging from these very rafters." With a nod, the Widow Sewall indicated upwards. Agnes followed her stare.

"And so, she wasn't often mentioned again. This town, Agnes, fears the wrong type of witchcraft. The blessings of spring are complicated, are they not? Some girls help the crops to grow, others manifest us good weather in spring, and some bless us with their gifts of song. Your mother wasn't stupid when she told you to hide your gift. But know this: the Widow Pluck knows what your gift is. The Grothi probably doesn't. He is a man obsessed with his own reflection." As if lost in thought, the Widow Sewall stopped talking, her eyes glazing over slightly. Agnes cleared her throat.

"So, you are here to tell me that…the Widow Pluck knows what we did, and knows my gift? What am I to do with this information?" she asked, her throat now sore, as though she had been the one speaking all along.

"You are to be careful. To bring your child into this world without so much as a murmur. If you displease these men—" the Widow glanced at the closed door briefly and then back again, leaning forward and lowering her voice, "they will denounce you as a witch. The Widow Pluck is very good at keeping herself and her position safe, and she will have no hesitation in denouncing you. But if you do not give her a reason to, she will not. For she knows that she has helped Saskia in a similar, albeit perhaps more ethical, way."

With a flourish, the Widow Sewall pulled up her hood and stood. She grabbed her basket and held it out. "A cabbage, if you please. If I am to leave with anything, it should be what I am owed." Agnes nodded, standing herself and hustling to the space beneath the sink, from which she pulled a browning cabbage.

"I take my leave."

"Wait, Widow Sewall. Wait," Agnes said suddenly, holding out her hand. "Why would the Gods gift me with a blessing that could be suspected as witchcraft? If they know that this is what the town—"

"Oh, child. The Gods play with the lives of mortals. They create the good and the bad and all that nestles here. Some of us mortals attempt to play the Gods, of course, but only if we are prepared to bargain for the ever after, when life is done with."

Agnes pulled her hand back, and opened the door, curtseying as the Widow left. She had indeed bargained: a child for her reputation, her word for the Widow Sewall's life. The bargain was a costly one, and now that she knew her father-in-law was aware of life's possibilities, and capable of such acts against a woman he loved, she would have to be even more careful.

MAELANC AUTUMN

Chapter Twenty-Five

The baby was growing. Agnes could feel it shifting inside her, night after night. The heavy sun of summer was starting to wane, replaced by the threat of autumn. The men kept working, Silo pulling the leather hard in the midday heat, murmuring to himself. The stones had started to be delivered to Saskia's new pitch, and each time a new delivery arrived, word spread through the town like liquid seeping under doors.

Pa had said almost nothing to Agnes over the last few weeks, and she had done her best to stay away from him, adding extra bits to his dishes when Silo wasn't watching, trying to sweeten him to her. Gone was the gentle hand that guided her into the household as she entered. In its place, suspicion reigned.

It was market day, and Agnes kicked the dry flakes of old mud from her boots as she walked, noticing that her stomach was now trying to hide them from her. It was not succeeding, but the effort was there. For the last few weeks, each time she had needed to go to market, Silo had stopped her. He had caught her at the gate, taken her basket from her, and told her to be more careful with their money. Turnips would have to do; they could get more from the oats. He warned her of being greedy while with child, suggesting that she was visiting the market in a state of hunger. This morning, though, she knew she would have no problems. Silo was taking some wares to a leather worker who was in town on a visit, leaving Pa behind. Agnes felt a jolt of glee as she passed the old gate without issue, her feet light beneath her.

The market was busy, the sunshine trickling through the paths, discussions and arguments, bartering and pleas filling the air. Agnes paused at the grocers, seeing a familiar-shaped head pulled back in laughter. It was the long silver hair of Saskia's mother, expertly braided as ever. As though sensing Agnes, she turned slowly, and her laughter turned into a sour smile.

"Ah, it is the tanner's wife," she said, "come to market at last. You've not been out in a while, have you?"

Agnes placed a hand over her stomach, though why, she wasn't sure. The matriarch's gaze lowered, and she nodded knowingly.

"I suppose you have heard my daughter's news? She, too, is with child, blessed by the Grothi. In celebration, her Finn is building her a house of stone." She turned back to the grocer and nodded conspiratorially. "A house of stone! A fine thing indeed. Still," she faced Agnes again to add, "we cannot all be so lucky. How are your parents?"

The stream of questions was coming thick and fast. The woman didn't even seem to notice that Agnes hadn't yet answered. She opened her mouth to speak but found herself flanked by the strong scent of honey. Turning, she saw Saskia was now standing beside her, more vibrant than she had ever seen her. It was as though she was reborn, not at all the woman who had spoken so desperately only weeks ago.

"Saskia! You look so well, I was—" Agnes began.

"You were worried? Well, sweet though it is, your concern was misplaced." With a flourish, the golden woman pulled aside her cloak, brandishing a bump that rivalled Agnes' in size. Agnes did not understand. The sight of it made the bile rise to her throat once more, and her stomach began to dance beneath her, bubbling under her skin.

"You...you look—" Agnes started, trying to think of a polite way to ask how it was possible that she was so developed.

"It turns out my sweet Saskia was merely confused. The baby was only hiding. Isn't that right, my love?" her mother said, sweeping the conversation from them.

"That's right, Mother."

Agnes stared. She had taken the hair to the Widow Sewall, had done what she had asked. She had taken the baby and it was inside her now. The Widow Pluck must have been powerful indeed to restore what had been taken.

"I see, well. Congratulations," Agnes answered, trying to keep her voice calm and level. The women smiled tightly at her, as though they knew that she was somehow to blame for whatever confusion had taken place. But why would they blame her, Agnes wondered, when the thought alone was so ridiculous? Clearly, the Widow Sewall had done nothing, engineering a situation where Agnes had fallen for her lies. The hair bristled on the back of Agnes' neck. She was with child, yes, but it was Silo's child all along. Her stomach roiled beneath her, sickness flushing back up through her throat. Her mouth filled, and she pushed her hand over her lips, trying to seal the liquid within.

"Oh, my goodness, Agnes, if you're unwell, you must step away from the food!" Saskia's mother barked, and Agnes stepped back in response, turning to run. Another surge came from her gut, and the seal broke as she forced herself away from the market square, leaving a trail behind her.

Chapter Twenty-Six

The door was answered almost immediately, and the Widow Sewall looked unlike she had before. Gone was the professional welcome, the carefully selected cloak. In its place, the Widow stood, dressed in a threadbare shawl and grey dress.

"Agnes! You look—"

"Sick," Agnes completed the sentence, her rage propelling her through the door. The Widow Sewall stepped aside, a look of dim amusement on her face.

"I did not expect you, which is unusual in itself. You have come from the market?"

Agnes sat before the fire, glancing down at her old dress. The front was stretching across her bump, the stains of nausea reflecting her place in society. She grimaced at the sight and looked back to the Widow, who was now stirring a cup of broth, eyebrows raised expectantly.

"Yes," Agnes said, "I have come from the market, where I saw Saskia and her mother."

"I see."

"You lied to me," Agnes accused her, the words stretching into the room and settling between the two women. The Widow frowned and sat before Agnes, her head cocked to one side in curiosity.

"Lied to you? I told you Saskia was with child."

"She is as far along as myself. She is…she says that she never lost a baby, and that means that I didn't gain her baby. You lied to me, Widow Sewall, so that I would give you my word. This is mine and Silo's, it has nothing to do with Saskia at all." Agnes placed her hands over her stomach as punctuation, staring at the Widow with a fierceness that seemed to make the Widow smile.

"Ah, you have come to the wrong conclusion, Agnes. It is an easy mistake—"

"How could it be a mistake? There's no explanation for Saskia being as far along as myself."

Silence took a seat between the two women once more, and the Widow Sewall let out a bright sigh before taking a sip of her drink. "Well, I dare say you will think this until the child is born. I myself know the truth of the matter. Agnes, you appear to have a gift for ridding yourself of the support in your life. Have you noticed? Regardless, I shall ask you to leave and to bear in mind that you shall still be beholden to our deal. I estimate you have a few months left, a winter child, unfortunately. I'll visit you then to clarify your error." With this, the Widow stood, indicating towards the door.

Agnes glared at her, standing up sharply. "When it is proven to be my child, I expect not to see you again," she muttered.

The Widow shook her head slowly, her expression still curiously unbothered. "Agnes, remember your place, dear. Do not bind your hands so tightly that you cannot accept a gift."

The child thudded in Agnes' stomach, responding to the words. A gift.

*

By the time Agnes arrived home, the rain had begun. Though the summer sun shone bright through the glorious seasons, the rain would always come at the end of summer. As Agnes stepped through the dripping water, she watched the town hustle and rush under cover, saw Saskia's stones be covered by oilskin, as though they could be damaged. Now, she sat in the kitchen beside the burgeoning fire and, in damp irritation, began to prepare a stew for supper. As she stirred fresh vegetables, the door creaked open.

"The rain is stopping me from doing my work," Pa said, his voice arriving before his footsteps. Agnes didn't turn, listening instead for Silo's movement. It didn't come. The door closed, and Agnes heard her father-in-law drop onto a stool.

"The rain has come early," he said into the silence, the bubbling of the pot punctuating his words. "How is the child?"

Agnes closed her eyes and breathed in the deeply savoury scents, the spiced air flitting in front of her nose. The baby responded with gentle murmurs beneath her skin.

"It is well, Pa," she responded, placing her hand over her stomach.

"Good. While my son is away, I thought I would take the... occasion, to talk to you. I know what you can do."

Agnes stared at the fire and felt her body tense, her shoulders squeezing upwards about her neck, the muscles flexing as though they attempted to strangle her. What would Pa do if she clarified his words by selecting a coal and turning on her stool? She swivelled on her chair and opened her mouth to speak. Her lips held together as though stuck, the skin stretching as she tried to move her tongue. She lifted her fingers to her mouth, touching its shape. There was nothing there, nothing to stop her from speaking. Pa looked at her expectantly. Agnes breathed in through her nostrils, trying not to panic.

"Do you hear the words I am saying, Agnes?" Pa said firmly, his brow creasing.

Agnes nodded. She tried to speak again but couldn't get her mouth to open.

"Insolent girl." His hand fell onto the table with force, as though trying to splinter the wood. Agnes reached for the ladle, stirring the stew. As she stirred, she could feel her mouth unstick, as if the steam were loosening a thread.

"Pa, will you have one ladle or two?" she whispered aloud, testing her ability to make sound.

"Two. And save some for your husband. He'll be home late."

Agnes nodded, pouring from the ladle into a bowl. She handed it to Pa, who took it gruffly, his politeness of her first visit now gone. In silence, they ate together, Agnes' mouth opening to accept the stew. Had it ever been sealed?

As she collected the bowls at the end of the meal, trying to avoid the hard stare of Pa, she briefly heard the quietest of noises above the crackling of the fire.

"Agnes…"

Chapter Twenty-Seven

The stone house was built quickly, blossoming before the autumn trees as if making fun of them for their loss of leaves. It was out of place among the wooden houses, flirting with the people of the town, showing them what privilege truly looked like. Agnes imagined the yellow flowers following with grace, bright bursts of sunshine illuminating the front of the stone. She stood before it, staring. Her shawl was wrapped tightly around her shoulders, her basket resting over her bump. As she watched, curious at the curved shape of the front door, it suddenly opened. Out walked Finn, his hair now grown a little, threatening to fall into one eye and yet somehow always remaining clear. He saw Agnes and smiled a bright grin, nodding.

"A fine house, is it not, Agnes?" he asked, his voice liquid.

She nodded. What words could she say? The house was grand. Everyone knew it.

"A fine gift for my wife. How fare the men in your house?"

Agnes tried not to stare, knowing instinctively that somewhere behind the windows before her sat Saskia, watching. Her bump would be blossoming, a waft of honey surrounding her head like a halo.

"Silo and his father do well, thank you," Agnes replied, without going into detail. There was no detail she might be willing to share.

"Yes. It's a shame you don't have a woman about the house to help with the child when it comes. We are blessed, I suppose. Although, you have your mother down yonder."

Silence wove its way between the two, and Agnes looked down at her basket, filled with brittle sprigs of heather she'd gathered at dawn. She had begun to weave the bed for the baby in the evenings, taking care to choose heather that was already drying, so that it wouldn't rot beneath its body. Of course, had she still been welcome at her parents' house, she might have been gifted the old crib that she once lay in, in which her brother had rested before her. The irony wasn't lost on her—this fragile cradle, so unlike the sturdy wooden crib she might have once dreamed of inheriting. That crib, lovingly crafted by an eager father, now felt as distant as her family's warmth. Her fingers hesitated over the heather, suddenly unsure of the point. What had she gained, if not her family? The cold comfort of a reputation, perhaps.

Finn cleared his throat. "Well, I must off. Tell Silo I send my greetings. The Widow Pluck will be making a special visit to Saskia in a month or so to check on her progress. I'm just telling you in case you...wanted to visit too? I don't want the silliness of the Spring Feast to come between our growing families, Agnes. You and Saskia have always been friends, as have Silo and myself. Why, his mother used to feed me at her very table."

Agnes glanced at Finn, curious at his words. "Silo's mother?" she asked, her tone carefully neutral, despite the sudden racing of her heart.

"Silo's stepmother," Finn responded, lifting his hand to wave at the window before him. Agnes glanced up, following his gaze, and saw that Saskia stood, window open, golden hair blowing in the breeze. Her skin was glowing, her eyes bright. It was like looking directly at a deity.

"His stepmother, who died," Agnes said as they both stared at the shining woman. Finn glanced sideways at her, delicate brow creasing.

"Yes, Agnes." With that, he turned, gave a final wave to his wife, and walked away. Agnes looked back to Saskia and watched her face drop. She stared back, before leaning forward and closing the window firmly. Agnes glanced up at the clouds moving over, threatening to rain on her heather.

Chapter Twenty-Eight

Autumn brought rotten leaves and heavy chill, covering the house in a fresh darkness. To Agnes, it was merely an extension of the quickening beneath her expanding skin. Silo and Pa discussed the changing weather with grumbles and hisses, declaring that autumn was a foul time to be alive.

"Emberfest is late this year," Silo whispered into his oats one morning, glaring at the dim light that dressed the doorway. "There will be no celebration worth having."

Agnes looked at her breakfast and swallowed the regular morning bile that accompanied her thoughts. "It should be nice to celebrate. The Grothi will be preparing the field," she responded, feeling Silo's sharp gaze upon her. He often stared at her this way now, as if he suspected her of planning something without his knowledge.

"We'll start moving the skins in tonight, son," Pa said, the only words that had left his lips so far that day. Silo nodded.

"Moving the skins in?" Agnes asked, raising her eyes.

"Yes. You keep the fire burning in that hearth all day long. It has to be used to some good," Pa replied.

"You're going to move the animal skins into this room? But there's hardly...space." Agnes looked around, her throat contracting. She knew how the outhouse smelled, knew that the skins were potent after their initial dousing in urine, before they had been dunked in the stream for a second time.

"Then make space," Pa spat, his bottom lip quivering, as though he were a small child demanding attention. "It's a blessing you have joined a family that doesn't baulk at feeding you."

Agnes felt her face harden, impossible to pull it back from a glare. With abandon, she began to speak, to say what she thought about her own kitchen being filled with such an unholy mess. "I don't—" As quickly as the words formed, they stopped. Agnes tried again, finding her tongue lying flat inside her mouth. She pushed, trying to lift it up, to make a noise. Silo and Pa watched her, curious.

"You don't...what?" Silo said eventually, sitting back on his stool to watch her struggle.

Agnes shook her head, changing her mind about the words. What would happen if she spoke them? She had already lost her original family, and the people of Locklear were nothing if not indifferent to her. She tried again, to say something new. "I don't mind," she said, pushing a spoonful of oats between her lips. The porridge was burned again. And yet, no one had mentioned it.

*

"Emberfest shall be held inside the church this year due to the rain," the Grothi began, his words dancing between the ears of his loyal congregation. "As we gather from the rich soil and bring to the feast, prepare yourself for sharing. The rain has ruined some of your neighbours' crops, so your graciousness will be accepted. In the manner of our autumn tradition, we will choose one child of spring to be our talisman."

Agnes shivered, the air closing in around her. She had never been selected and knew that with her low standing in Locklear, she never would be. Her spring blessing was of little importance to the Grothi, and she knew it was best to keep it that way.

"Your talisman for this year has been named. Saskia, come join us at the front."

Agnes frowned. Saskia was not a child of spring, and her gift was nonsense. As far as she could see, she hadn't even matched anybody in love since Agnes herself, and that could not be said to be a great match. She looked around her, trying to catch eyes with anyone else, to ascertain whether these thoughts had occurred to the others. Everyone seemed satisfied with the choice, their eyes watching Saskia slip from the aisle, her bump stretching the flowing cream material that moved about her, her hair braided down her back. She was wearing dried lavender in her hair, Agnes noticed, an extra touch, as if she knew she would be called to the front.

Saskia reached the Grothi and dipped her head, one hand protectively placed on her stomach. The Grothi smiled widely, one hand turned to the front of the church, and let out a large chuckle. It was a strange, mirthless noise that filled Agnes' ears.

"What better talisman can there be for the year than a child of spring who is so blessed? Those of you who watch the comings and goings of visitors may have seen Saskia's new dwelling, which lifts this village from the earth and into the stars. May we all one day aspire to be so grateful to the Gods. Our gracious thanks provide their love, as Saskia has shown us. Throughout this year, she will be your source for all things luck and prayer."

Saskia turned to the crowd and smiled gently, her eyes just lifting beneath their lids. She was the picture of gracious benevolence, and despite being grateful that it wasn't her being chosen, Agnes felt an overwhelming urge to scream.

"Thank you all, and thank you, as ever, to the Gods. I am so grateful to be your talisman. You must feel free to–" she continued, and Agnes felt the skin beneath her dress start to pucker and flinch. The baby began to move violently, kicking hard for the first time. With a moan, she leaned forward, holding a hand over her stomach, wishing to quiet the child.

"And to my wives with child, we are in this journey together. I shall be starting a mother's group from winter, and together, we shall raise our–"

The baby slammed into Agnes' pelvis, sick crashing up her oesophagus and into her mouth.

"Thank you, Saskia," the Grothi said, stepping forward once more. The baby stopped moving almost instantly. Agnes swallowed the sick, sitting back into the pew, and glanced around. One of the wives beside her narrowed her eyes at her, and Agnes looked away hurriedly. As Saskia walked back down the aisle, she caught eyes with Agnes, her pale green irises pausing at her bump.

"You should feel welcome to join us, Agnes," she said as she passed, leaning in.

Before Agnes could think, sick covered the back of the pew in front. The rest of the wives squealed, recoiling in horror, and Agnes stood, noting Silo's expression as she left the congregation behind. It wasn't one of pity, pain, or anguish. It was one of barely contained expectation.

Chapter Twenty-Nine

Traditionally, Agnes and her family had always avoided Emberfest. They had picked apples and sent them to the church, showing their support and manifesting a second harvest, as with the rest of the community, but when it came to attendance, they stayed indoors. Her mother had often cited the mud, saying that the feet in the field churned it, leaving her with more work once they arrived home. Agnes had always suspected that it was more than that, though. Most of the women came to Emberfest with a flourish, wearing an item of clothing they had been making over the previous winter period. Agnes' mother told her that they didn't have the luxury of personal projects and that the only things that mattered were staying warm and keeping food on the table. How did the other families have time for both, Agnes would ask. The answer would never come, but it was clear what it was. Sacrifice.

The kitchen was now filled with skins, and the scent of the room was something Agnes was certain she could never get used to. As she woke in the morning, it drifted up the stairs, pausing in front of her nose, teasing and winding its way through her. It burned her throat as she lit the fire, and she breathed the smoke into her lungs, grateful for an escape.

It was the day of Emberfest, and Agnes had woken a little early, unsure if the family would be joining in. She was still determining what their traditions were, not wanting to insult Silo's godliness by asking. The familiar tread on the stairs told her that her husband was on his way down. *Creak. Thump. Creak. Thump.*

"Wife, pull together some things for Emberfest. Turnips, a couple of cabbages. No one will be expecting much from us with the condition you are in. The Grothi has announced that as the rain has stopped, so we shall be celebrating in the field. The Gods have seen our plight." His voice arrived before Agnes could turn, and she nodded as she stood.

"What sort of items do you usually take?" she asked, smiling at him, perhaps the first smile she had offered in a week.

"What I have just mentioned."

"Of course. Perhaps your stepmother offered something more, such as dried flowers?"

Silo stopped mid-reach for a calfskin and glanced at Agnes, his face the picture of surprise. "I'm sorry?"

"Your stepmother." The repetition felt like a finger pressing on her throat, pushing against her skin. "Perhaps she took something else?"

At that moment, Pa entered the room, wearing his smartest trousers, patched up only over one knee. "What's all this?" he asked, his voice low. Clearly, his ears were better than his age allowed.

"Agnes is asking after my stepmother and the things that she brought to Emberfest," Silo said, eyes glaring at the floor. He knew. Agnes could see from his expression that he knew exactly what had happened to the woman.

"Agnes?" Pa said, "Why would you be asking that?"

Agnes opened her lips to quell the suspicion, to say that it was simply polite, wanting to carry on the family's great traditions, and nothing to do with anything. Once more, her tongue fell flat in her mouth, heavy, as if it could not be lifted.

"Agnes." The word sprang through the air, neither of the men's mouths moving. With effort, Agnes turned towards the fire, leaning forward and stoking the flames. From the crackling, she heard an instruction as clear as though it had been spoken from her own mouth.

"Agnes, hold your tongue."

The townspeople of Locklear came out in force, their woollen winter cloaks folded into their belts to keep the mud from creeping up the material. Smiles were shared with one another, root vegetables given as gifts, hessian bunting dictating which part of the field joy was consigned to.

The Grothi sat on a special wooden stage above the mud. Agnes carried her basket, stepping behind Silo and Pa. The walk there had been in silence, and since their lack of discussion that morning, Agnes had decided not to bring up the stepmother again. At least not when Pa was in the room. There was something strange in the air when he confronted her about anything. It was as though someone was holding a hand over her mouth, forbidding her to speak.

"Silo!" Finn trotted over to the small group, reaching his hand out warmly for his friend. Behind him, Saskia blossomed and bloomed, her basket overflowing with turnips, radishes, and even a white pumpkin. Agnes stared, unflinching. With a sharp smile, they came to pause in front of each other, their stomachs the exact same size.

"Agnes, you came. For the life of me, I could not remember a time that you and your family had ever joined us at Emberfest."

Agnes nodded, selecting a turnip from her basket and passing it to Saskia, taking glee in the fact that it bore mud. "Here, a gift."

"Well, thank you," Saskia responded, taking the turnip and gently resting it among her varied goods. "How kind people have been. I suppose that's the response to being the talisman!"

Agnes breathed in deeply, inhaling the honeyed scent. She knew what she wanted to say, that it was ridiculous, Saskia being the talisman, that she wasn't even a child of spring. But, try as she might, the words would not form fully in her mouth, so she smiled instead.

"Have you ever been the talisman, Agnes?" Saskia asked sweetly, as if such a thought were viable. It wasn't. Saskia knew that beyond everything that stood in Agnes' way, her brother forsaking the family's reputation, Agnes' own slip-ups in pride, there was nothing within Agnes that the people of the town turned to. She wasn't particularly bright, wasn't a magnet for ideas and thoughts and discussions. She was the tanner's wife. That's all she was. Saskia, on the other hand, seemed to draw people to her. Even now, as she stood with her basket gently slung over her arm, Agnes could see the people of the town glancing over every now and then, as if she were the sun.

"No, Saskia," Agnes replied. It had never even occurred to her, had never been something on her mind or even in her periphery. Now, as she stood in front of the honeyed woman of Locklear, the talisman of their fortune, she wanted it. The realisation caught her like a wasp sting, pricking at her skin, puckering the swollen shape before her. Did she only want what Saskia had? A gift that was no gift at all, different from the ability to touch fire without being burned, hidden from the world. A husband with good looks, a sweet scent, a stone house. A child that didn't push against her insides until it made her vomit. With a nod, she watched Saskia and her husband swan away across the field, noticing that Silo and Pa had walked off as well, leaving her behind.

*

The day continued with dancing and prayer. Agnes joined in as much as Silo and Pa would allow, which was little. At one point, Silo looked so bored that Agnes wondered if they might not have benefitted more from sitting at home among the skins, watching the sun rise and fall in the sky.

Upon the stage, the Widow Pluck sat beside Saskia and the Grothi, watching the festivities with a glum smugness. Saskia's mother moved about the crowd with a large, newly threaded basket, vegetables overflowing, placing items in other hands with genial smiles.

Beneath her skin, the baby kicked, and as Agnes watched the crowd throb and ebb, she felt a presence beside her. Without turning, she knew exactly who it was.

"Not long to go now." Agnes turned to the voice and saw the Widow Sewall looking, for all intents and purposes, like a regular Locklear resident. Her cloak was clean, her hair braided, and her basket full.

"No, not long now," Agnes responded, looking back to the crowd. She noticed the Widow Pluck glancing over, her eyes pausing on the pair. "I am surprised to see you here, Widow Sewall."

"I brave Emberfest for the food. You have prepared?" the Widow asked, picking up a cabbage and placing it in Agnes' basket, a strange gift which felt too symbolic.

"I have created the crib," Agnes sighed, thinking of the sad, lopsided little basket that waited in the bedroom at home.

"It is enough for the physical child, perhaps."

There was a lull as Agnes listened to this sentence again in her mind.

"And the...spiritual?" She glanced over at the Widow, a frown settling across her brow.

"Yes, the spiritual. That's always the thing to be careful of, isn't it?" The Widow nodded at the stage, and Agnes turned to see that the Widow Pluck was walking towards them. Her expression had rested in a gentle smile.

"Sister," the Widow Sewall said, nodding her head.

"Sister," Pluck responded. She looked at Agnes, then down at her stomach, her eyes settling for a moment too long. "Not long to go. I dare say you will have the child out in the world soon enough."

"Sister, we were just discussing the spiritual protection of the children of Locklear. What might you suggest for Agnes and her child?" the Widow Sewall asked, her voice strong and defiant.

"Spiritual protection?" Pluck's eyes lingered on Agnes'. "This concerns you?"

Agnes opened her mouth to speak but found her voice muffled by Sewall's answer. "It concerns all new mothers."

"Does it? Saskia is due around the same time, and it does not seem to concern her so much. But, if the occasion calls for it, here is my advice. Keep in touch with your Grothi, for his work speaks directly to the Gods. You do not have that power, and that is what your Grothi is for. Bring up your child to speak to the Grothi every week, every Sunday. Avoid temptations. Show your child that the blessing of spring is the type of magic we adhere to in these lands. Other things can be sought, with ease, but the cost is great," the Widow Pluck paused on the last words, as if savouring them. Then, she leaned forward and lowered her voice. "You do not need to look far for proof of this cost. Stick to your duties, keep your thoughts to yourself, and raise an obedient child. Through this, their spiritual side will bloom." She ran her eyes across Agnes, pausing at the hands holding the basket. Agnes followed her gaze and saw that her skin had started to flush, small red bumps forming across her knuckles. As if the Widow Pluck's sight had power, they began to itch.

"Ah, you suffer with your pregnancy, Agnes. Try camomile on those, but do not be surprised if it spreads." With a curt nod, the Widow Pluck turned, heading back towards the stage.

The Widow Sewall made a small noise of amusement, a hum that flitted up at the end, almost invisible to the ear. With this, she plucked the cabbage from Agnes' basket, placed it in her own, and wandered off.

FLEGMAT WINTER

Chapter Thirty

Once Emberfest had passed, the men had gone back to work, the kitchen remained full of the strong scent of skins, and Agnes fell into a regular pattern. In the mornings, she would let her hands soak in camomile, trying to stop the itch that had begun to plague her. She would make the water as hot as possible, knowing that she could not feel the heat and that such a sensation seemed to be the only thing to calm the irritation.

She barely left the house, waking, sweeping, feeding the men, and trying desperately not to listen to the near-daily mention of her name. That, too, had become a pattern.

Whenever she rested alone, in front of the fire, her name was spoken. If she reached for the coals, her old amusing pastime, it became more urgent, a warning tone causing fear to prickle in her throat. And when Pa asked her a question, more often than otherwise, she found she couldn't answer. She was caught between the men's expectant stares, as they wondered why she didn't speak up when her name was spoken. But she had, and if she kept answering when the two men didn't hear what she so clearly did, the consequences could be dire. She knew this. It was threaded within the Widow Pluck's warning to keep her thoughts to herself.

They were all signs of what Agnes knew already. The baby was trying to punish her. It knew, and its knowledge was seeping out of her skin, of her mouth, and holding down her tongue.

After weeks of the pattern, her stomach expanding before her, the day came. Agnes woke in the middle of the night, her stomach sore and strange. Silo had recognised the need for more than one chamber pot in the bedroom, something he was previously against (which seemed strange to Agnes, given the stench of his profession), and as Agnes knelt on the floor, she realised that she had made a grave error.

"Silo!" she hissed through the night air, her stomach pulsating beneath her. "Silo! Wake up!"

He groaned and rolled over before sitting up in bed and focusing lazily on her form. "What?"

"I think it's time. I think you should go and fetch—" Pain radiated up Agnes' spine, pushing against her pockmarked skin. She stared down at her stomach, stretching against the material of her nightgown, and felt her arms prickle and pop with intense itching. Her stomach was a blister, waiting to burst. She bit her tongue.

"Who?"

"The Grothi! The Widow Pluck! My mother!" Whether any of these were correct, Agnes did not know, but she felt the need for someone else besides the men that she lived with. Even the Grothi, with his sour and static ways, would be an improvement.

With a sigh, Silo climbed out of bed and pulled on his trousers and boots, leaving the room without a word. Agnes heard him descend the steps, the front door slamming and rattling the house.

She groaned, leaning forward, feeling her stomach contract as though it were a chicken's foot. What should she be doing? Her brain felt empty, and quailing, Agnes saw the reality of what had not been done in the preceding months. She hadn't asked how you were supposed to have a baby.

"Agnes."

The voice. With a shudder, she answered. "Yes."

"Agnes, to the kitchen, prepare a tincture of sugar and vinegar." The sentence was the fullest that Agnes had heard from the voice, and yet it was quieter still, almost an echo of a thought.

With a deep breath, Agnes pulled herself up, using the bedframe and saw that she had left a pool of liquid behind her, seeping through the wooden floorboards. Her first thought was that Silo would be enraged to see it so, and yet she found no space within her heart to care. With great caution, she made it down the stairs and to the kitchen, hearing not a sound from Pa up above.

Beneath the sink lay the vinegar. Agnes had no sugar. The mere mention of it would, ordinarily, have made her laugh, for such a thing was bestowed on royalty. With a sharp breath inward, Agnes searched for what she did have.

"I have nothing like sugar here," she whispered into the air, hoping for a response.

"Honey," came the response. With a grimace, Agnes rubbed her forehead, finding sweat beads lingering there. There was no honey. The scent of it was too much, it pulled at her tongue, forcing sickness from within. It meant Saskia.

A rage began at the base of her stomach, flickering upward in licking movements, filling her lungs and chest with an anger she had never felt. She leaned forward, kneeling on the floor, letting the feeling take over her body. With haste, she opened the vinegar bottle. The scent of the sour wine dissipated into the air and, for a moment, made it better, clouding the smell of urine and stripped-back leather, the loud odour of a tanner's house. Agnes dipped her finger in the bottle and sucked it, her taste buds buckling and bolting at the strange sudden flavour, the baby kicking and squirming within. It was coming. It was now.

The door slammed open, and in walked Silo, flanked by someone Agnes had not asked for. It was the Widow Sewall. With a grimace, Agnes let out a groan, rage still lit within.

"What is she doing here?" she yelled into the air, the cold wind battling with the visitor's cloak.

"The Grothi, the Widow Pluck…they are tending to Saskia. She is in labour also," Silo said plainly, his eyes flicking to Sewall. "Your mother would not answer the door, would not come."

The Widow stepped forward, closing the door behind her. "I am the one you have here, child. Come now, let's put that anger to good use, shall we?" With the flicker of a smirk, she turned to Silo. "Away with you. You are not welcome here."

Silo looked unreservedly relieved at this turn of events and rushed up the staircase, two steps at a time. The Widow stepped forward and pulled the pot above the fire towards her, hastily building the flames beneath it. Once done, and it was crackling in the grate, she drew a couple of tinctures from her cloak and poured them in, stirring and singing. What the words of the song were, Agnes could not tell.

Agnes watched as quietly as she could, leaning backwards on the floor. She could see now, strangely, that she had done a poor job with the sweeping, the dust on the hearth was thick, and beneath the table it lay heavy. Her stomach was still pounding and thudding.

Eventually, the Widow Sewall turned and poured the contents of the pot into a cup, handing it to Agnes. Without even questioning what was inside, she drank deeply. It tasted of lavender and fresh sunshine, a far cry from the room she found herself lying in. She closed her eyes and breathed in, inhaling the scents of something new, something better. A driving force began to pulsate from her chin to midriff and then beyond.

"Focus on driving it out, Agnes."

Agnes opened her eyes and stared at the woman before her, who now knelt on the floor.

"Push." The word came, but the Widow's mouth did not move. Agnes felt that rage again and, with a silent scream, allowed her body to do what it was asking.

In a burst, the baby arrived. Agnes felt it leave her like a great weight, the relief a stinging. Whatever the Widow had given her to drink had dulled her senses, made her feel lightheaded, but she focused hard on the woman before her. She held a lump, nodding, and then passed it over to Agnes.

Agnes stared. The baby was not covered in blood, as she had thought it would be, but honey. Its skin was thick with the gooey liquid, golden and sweet to her nostrils. She breathed in, disbelief reverberating through her senses. The child had a small nose, delicate features. Atop its head lay a mop of golden hair. Agnes swallowed, looking down. It was a boy. He opened his eyes in that moment and fixed a juddery gaze on her own. In an instant, he screamed.

Chapter Thirty-One

Silo was pleased, Pa relieved. The child had arrived, and he was a male. After the Widow Sewall had cleaned the baby, swaddled it, and handed it back to its mother, she leaned in close to her ear.

"It seems you were wrong. This child has nothing of you about it." With that, she stood, wished Silo hearty congratulations, and left.

Agnes stared at the child, who now slept in her arms. He still smelled strongly of honey, and with every slight movement or whimper he made, the scent hit the back of Agnes' throat like a stone.

"What will we name him?" Silo asked, his face glowing. He was proud, delighted that he had produced a male, an heir. Agnes looked around the pelt-filled kitchen, wondering what sort of kingdom this was to be an heir to. Silo leaned forward, and almost instinctively, Agnes began to lean back, unsure of his intent. With a wry smile, he kissed her on the forehead and then nodded.

"We shall call him Godwin."

Godwin. Agnes stared back at the child and mouthed the word, not saying it aloud. It was one that the Grothi would be delighted with, no doubt.

"A strong name, Son. Well done, Agnes. You have brought a male heir into the house, and he will grow strong and wise, able to carry on the family business." Pa stood with his hands on his hips, his chin high and proud.

"Thank you," Agnes whispered in response, unsure what she should be doing now. Should she make breakfast? The sun was already high in the sky, and it was surely almost lunchtime. Would she be allowed back to bed? Her skin ached from the act of giving birth, the place between her legs sore. She noticed, with mild surprise, that her skin was no longer itchy. The red bumps had now softened to marks, almost indistinguishable from the space around them. She looked to Silo, clearing her throat. Before she could speak, he opened his mouth.

"Wife, I shall fetch the Grothi directly. Today is not a day for working, for today, we celebrate Godwin. Tell me, what would you like to eat?"

Agnes almost laughed, the question sounding so bizarre in her ears. She had never been asked such a thing in her whole life. "I...I would like..." she began, desperately trying to think of foods. All that came into her mind was cabbage. "Cabbage. Cabbage stew," she said eventually, already disappointed in her decision.

Silo raised his eyebrows, clearly impressed with her restraint during such a time. "And so it will be. Pa, while I fetch the Grothi, visit the market, won't you?"

Pa pulled a face, brief, but apparent to Agnes, before quietly agreeing. With haste, the two men left, leaving Agnes and Godwin alone in the house.

"You are here now," Agnes said to the sleeping baby. He stirred, his eyes opening and half fixing on her own. She did not know how much he could see, but he wrinkled his nose as if sniffing her. "I do not know you, and you do not know me." Godwin stared as if silently agreeing. He opened his mouth, a small pink tongue dipping out and tasting the air. Agnes did not know what to do, so did nothing. As if realising then that this was not his mother, Godwin let out a loud cry. It shook the pelts of the house, and Agnes felt their shudders.

Her body began to tremble, from the skin upon her arms to her pelvis, a dull and persistent squeeze, just as she had felt before Godwin arrived. She held him tighter, breathing in the smoked air of the room, feeling the gaze of the child upon her. She was Mother. A liquid began to spread beneath her.

The Grothi arrived quickly, his face drawn and tired. Behind him, the Widow Pluck stood. She, too, was the image of exhaustion, and Agnes saw their noses crinkle against the smell of the room, their eyes lazily moving across the drying pelts. Pa was not yet back from the market, and Agnes' stomach was starting to gurgle with hunger.

"Silo tells us that you have birthed a boy, Godwin, into the town of Locklear," the Grothi began, spreading his hands wide. Agnes nodded, showing the whimpering child as though it were an example of what she had, indeed, done.

The Widow Pluck stepped forward and took Godwin gently, holding him in her arms. "You have fed him?" she asked. Agnes shook her head. No one had told her anything; nobody had said what he should eat, how she should feed him, or what to do with the child. He was just there, and then everyone had gone. Agnes was still sitting on the floor, afraid to move. The warmth beneath her, she was certain, would be honey.

"Agnes, has your mother given you any advice on how to care for the child?" The Widow Pluck frowned, glancing from the Grothi to Godwin.

Agnes shook her head in silence.

"And the Widow Sewall, who Silo says helped deliver Godwin...has she not informed you of the feeding?"

The gentleness of the questioning made Agnes want to burst into tears. It was as though the Widow was speaking to her like she was an idiot. Still, her ignorance and naivety suddenly felt like a great eagle digging its claws into her shoulder blades.

"I am sure that Agnes will learn as all mothers do, through experience," Silo said, his voice evaporating into silence.

"Well, it is a good thing that the talisman has proclaimed a group of mothers should come together at her new home. You will learn there, Agnes. In the meantime, once the Grothi has blessed your child, I shall give you the basics." The Widow Pluck tried a small smile, the expression sticking on her lips, entirely unnatural. She turned to the Grothi and presented the child. His eyes widened, his cheeks puckering as though he were biting the flesh inside them.

"Blessed Godwin, welcome to Locklear. Your father has prayed for you. We know that you will live a long and happy–" the baby let out a cry, and the Grothi shook his head as if that might push the noise away. "–life. The blessing has been completed. Pluck, if I may have a word with you outside?"

The Widow nodded, handing Godwin back to his mother. Together, the two left the house, and Agnes strained to hear the hushed voices of their discussion. After a moment, the Widow Pluck came back in.

"Silo, I shall be talking to your wife about things that a husband does not need to know. Perhaps you could go and find something else to do," the Widow said plainly, not seeming to notice Silo's eyes sharpening at her message. Agnes had never seen anyone speak to him in such a manner and she could see that even the day's glorious gift was no ointment for the insult.

"As you wish," he responded before stalking out of the door without a glance at his wife and child. Once he had gone, the Widow pulled up a chair before Agnes.

"You are aware that Saskia has given birth today, are you not?"

Agnes nodded; of course, she was. "It was the reason the Grothi and yourself could not attend my birth."

"Indeed it was. She has given birth to a girl."

Agnes nodded. It meant nothing to her, not really. Silo had hoped for a boy, and perhaps Finn had hoped for a girl. Such was life.

"Your child does not look much like you or the father, does he?" The Widow leaned forward, stroking Godwin's head with a single finger. Agnes looked down, surveying the scene. It was true; he did not. His golden hair was nothing like her own muddy colour, and his flesh was much paler than hers.

"No, but children grow and change," Agnes said. Did she believe the child was hers? She wasn't sure. It was true that he looked nothing like her, and the scent of him was gut-churning. But way back in the recess of her mind, she remembered something her mother had once told her: that being a parent was not all ease and bliss, that sometimes one could feel a lack of connection to a child. Perhaps that was all this was.

"Yes, Agnes, they do," the Widow responded. She said no more about it, launching into a description of the basics of child-rearing, feeding, and clothing. With exhausted ears, Agnes listened as closely as she could. Once the Widow had left her alone, and before Silo returned to her, Agnes stood carefully, her body flickering in pain. Behind her, she had left honey.

*

The baby breathed out softly. Godwin. His face was strange, not what Agnes had expected. But then, what had she expected? Perhaps eyes that hinted at what he had put her through. Not just the bile that continuously rose to her throat, but the weakness he had given her hair. When she was with child, it had felt glossier somehow, heavier on her head. Now, it was lanker still, greasy and unkempt, thinner than ever. When she looked at him, she saw the honey that he had been born covered in. Honey, not blood. And yet, the Widow Sewall had not mentioned it and not hinted that it was a strange thing. It appeared strange to Agnes, but what did she know? Godwin was the baby, her only one. His appearance, his face, and its complicated newborn lines were things that Agnes would never again be able to replicate.

"The baby sleeps," Pa said quietly as he shifted through the kitchen. Agnes glanced up, watching his back at the door. "They sleep a lot at this age. Perhaps an opportunity for you to get more done about the house, to sweep the hearth, clear out some of the old for the new." Without waiting for an answer, he left. The baby sleeps, she thought, in silent agreement. The baby seemed arrogant in his sleep. If she was unable to sleep for looking after him, what right did he have to sleep when being looked after? As she thought this, she laid a heavy head on the table and closed her eyes. Just for a moment.

Chapter Thirty-Two

The crying was everywhere. When it began, the squeal pulsated through the air, travelling to Agnes' ears like a foul wind and pushing against her eardrums with the force of the crier's eversticky hands. There was no getting away from it. Agnes tried everything she could think of. She sang loudly while sweeping the hearth, built the fire as large as possible so that the crackling might drown out the noise, wrapped a blanket about her head, covering her ears.

The child didn't seem to respond to Agnes' efforts. He pushed at her when she tried to pick him up to soothe him. He wrinkled his nose when she neared him, as if he couldn't bear the smell of her. And indeed, she found she could barely stand the scent of him, so strong was the odour of honey. It stuck and cloyed at the back of her throat, and in her desperation, she banned the substance from the house. Silo called her strange, tutted at her ever-expanding list of rules.

Feeding was a trial. After the Widow Pluck showed her how, she had attempted to do it alone. At first, Godwin would not latch on, staring at her as if he hated the very bones of her body. Or was that just in her head? When he looked at Silo, there was more recognition there, as if he were truly his father. But Agnes knew better.

It had been a week. A long, exhausting week of trying to understand this new world she lived in. Pa had generally been more absent than Agnes had ever noticed, and in his absence, the voice in the house began to quieten down. On occasion, when Godwin squealed his displeasure at the world, Agnes swore that she could hear a hushing accompanying the shrill noise, a quiet, dull breath of air.

"He is growing bigger," Silo said, peering into the handmade cot at the sleeping child, whom Agnes had just managed to put down. Sometimes, it was as though he cried for everything, for her holding him, for her putting him down, and beyond. She found herself standing at the in-between, a lost mother, refusing the title.

"He is, yes."

"And so, I thought we could take him to the tavern tonight. You have not been out since you gave birth, and my son would like to see the sights." Silo smiled, a new, increasingly interesting thing to Agnes. Though he did little to help her with the child, the mere existence of Godwin seemed to drive his mood upward.

Agnes breathed in sharply. The thought of going out was too much. The eyes of the town would be upon her, and they would know, wouldn't they? They would take one look at her child and know what she did. His skin was still tacky from the honey. Her skin was still delicate, as though a touch might break it. The sensations around her pelvis were ever present, not as sharp as they had been when Godwin had come into the world, but a silent reminder of his presence. To sit in front of other people, while trying to contain everything that her body now was, seemed to be a violent suggestion, a shudder of implausibility.

"No, no, it is too soon. It is too soon, Silo," she flustered, causing him to glance at her with curiosity.

"Too soon? It is not dangerous. Saskia has already taken her child to the tavern, with Finn beside her."

Agnes smoothed down her apron, feeling her stomach still protruding in the hangover of childbirth, and shook her head. "I don't want to," she whispered into the air. The words settled between them. With a start, she realised that it may have been the first time in a long time that she had truly said what she wanted. Silo paused, staring at the child as if he had noticed it too.

"If that's...how you feel. Perhaps next week." He gave her another smile, this one slightly sad, as if unsure whether he had said the right thing and, for some reason, caring.

Another week passed. Agnes had managed to avoid visiting the church with Silo and Pa, and they had relented, giving her the benefit of the doubt. The days were merging in a strange fluid motion, time like water, Agnes' thoughts knocking into each other. She watched Godwin, fed Godwin, swept, cleaned and ate. She counted the days, trying to make the scraps of food in the cupboard last, because the thought of going to the market was overwhelming.

Her body was healing. She saw the honey diminishing between her legs and felt her body's slow efforts to gain control. Swelling was still there. It lent her reminders daily.

"Agnes, there is but one turnip in the pot," Pa said on one particular morning. Agnes ran her eyes over him, seeing his slight frame. "Have you not been to the market?"

"I have not had time, Pa. Godwin is—"

"Godwin is a baby. He will go where you go. It is a time of learning, Agnes, and you must learn to exist with him." Pa stepped forward, his face softening. In the moment, Agnes felt like crying, like reaching out and grasping him in a hug. But she didn't dare. "Do you understand, child? As you embraced moving here, you must embrace Godwin."

Agnes nodded, her tongue heavy in her mouth. She stood still as Pa collected the basket, placing it on the ground beside the swaddled baby. With care, he lifted his supposed grandchild and placed him inside. "There. Now, it is cold out. Wear your woollen cloak, and please make sure you come back with a little meat. Our kindness is wearing as thin as our stomachs, Agnes."

Though his face was gentle, Agnes recognised a hesitant anger behind his eyes. It was there, present, a reminder that she was not truly her own woman. She laid a hand on the basket and breathed in. With care, she donned her cloak, careful to use a part of it to also cover the child.

"For warmth," she lied, stepping into the world.

*

The market was as busy as ever despite the cold weather of winter closing in. At first, Agnes kept her hood up, her head down, focusing only on the fogged air forming in front of her face. Every now and then, she glanced down at the child to find him sleeping still, as if the chilly air upon his cheeks pleased him.

The first stop was the butchers. The scent was overwhelming, but now that she had had the baby, she was able to go in again without feeling the need to vomit.

"Ah, you are back. It's been a while," the butcher said, a soft smile on his face. "And is that the baby?" he indicated to the basket, and Agnes nodded, moving her cloak so that it covered a little more of the child's face.

"A sweet child, no doubt." He wrapped up her request and threw in a few extra scraps, too, wrinkling his nose with faux delight. "For your strength."

Agnes took the package, placing it on top of the child's legs. Was that allowed? She had no idea. She just had to get out of there as soon as possible. As Agnes stepped into the hustle of the street, the noise she had been dreading sprang to her ears.

"Agnes!" her name travelled between the people, and in an instant, she knew. Agnes picked up her pace, walking as if she hadn't heard a thing. If she could get home with only the meat, that would be something. That would be enough of an accomplishment for the day, and Pa and Silo would be pleased.

"Agnes!" the voice came again. Ahead, the people of the market seemed to converge as if it were a pre-planned dance. Agnes knew she couldn't hold off any longer. With a deep sigh, she turned and focused on the woman striding towards her, a child bound to her chest. Saskia.

"There you are. I haven't seen you at all since you gave birth! Finn tells me that Silo has been at the tavern, that you've been doing fine. Why haven't you been to the church yet? The Grothi must see Godwin to bless him." She leaned forward, one hand gently moving her daughter's head to the side, to try and grab a glimpse of Godwin in his basket.

Silo said that she had been doing fine? A strange idea, when the man didn't know what had taken place within her body. As if responding to that thought, Agnes' stomach flickered. She moved her cloak, covering the baby's head lightly.

"He does not like the cold. Who is this?" Agnes asked, her eyes focusing on the back of a head she felt she knew all too well. Saskia's daughter had blonde hair, as could be expected, a crop of golden curls sprouting from a yellow root. Her body was wrapped up against the cold, and Saskia turned slowly to show the baby's face to Agnes. She tried desperately not to exclaim, not to mutter a word aloud. It was unmistakable. The child had the same fine features: the eyes, the nose...all of it. They had the same face.

"This is Ethelfleda," Saskia said proudly. "Isn't she beautiful?"

"Ethelfleda," Agnes said, repeating the word. She had never heard the name before, but it seemed to suit the child that gazed at her now. Suddenly, a gurgle reached her ears. She looked down to see that Godwin's face was now uncovered, and he was staring at Saskia with wide eyes, his face the picture of calm delight. It was an expression she had never seen on him before. He was entranced.

"We have to go," Agnes started, before seeing Saskia's eyes drop to the basket. Agnes couldn't be quick enough.

"Why he's..." Saskia began, making eye contact with Godwin. Agnes searched her face for the remaining words of the sentence, knowing exactly what they were.

"He's big," Agnes finished for her, pulling her cloak back around the basket and clearing her throat dramatically. Saskia's eyes were hard.

"He looks nothing like you," Saskia announced, her words gathered by the wind and whipped away from the women. Agnes nodded, looking back at Saskia's own baby.

"Hmm. Lucky for him. Perhaps I shall join your mother's meeting sometime, Saskia, but for now, I must depart."

Saskia nodded, taking up her skirts and turning away before Agnes could. Agnes watched her go for a moment. What could she suspect anyway? The thought was outrageous, outlandish. And all babies looked the same. Agnes felt eyes still on her and glanced around hesitantly, trying to focus on the sea of faces. Eventually, her eyes rested on her mother's, who stood a little way off. Agnes raised a hand. Her mother's face was thin, the bags beneath her eyes large. Without any sort of acknowledgement, she turned away.

Chapter Thirty-Three

The weight of motherhood pressed down on Agnes like a sodden cloak. How was she to raise a man? Her own mother had left her ill-equipped for such a task. Agnes found herself wondering about her brother—her mother's son—and where he might be now. Gone. The word echoed in the hollow spaces of her heart.

Godwin lay in his basket, a fragile creation in Agnes' inexperienced hands. His gaze, unwavering and inscrutable, bore into her. What was she expected to feel for the child? When she reached for emotion, all she could grasp were fading memories: her mother's gentle touch as she combed Agnes' hair, the secretive way she concealed her gift.

Godwin let out a sharp cry, a bleat for attention. She moved over to his basket, and upon seeing her face, the baby paused. His eyes, large and blue, too big for his small, fleshy, features, found her own. He blinked, and Agnes felt the weight of his silent appraisal. Though his countenance was so expressionless, Agnes knew what he felt, for it was the same as her own feelings.

Lack.

It cloaked them both, a shared inheritance.

Godwin's stare was a void, an absence so profound it became tangible.

Another bleat, only this time, tinged with accusation. Godwin watched, his squawks reminiscent of the crows that haunted the border of Locklear, their beady eyes tracking her every move. What did he expect? Save for an apology, a plea. A child born of winter to a child born of the spring.

Phlegm from blood.

"Agnes." The sound of her name made her start, and she watched the open mouth of Godwin, waiting for him to repeat the miracle. A crow had spoken her name.

A touch on her shoulder caused her to turn, facing her husband. In his hands, he held a cow horn, and in her confusion, Agnes stared.

"Agnes. It is a gift from Saskia and Finn."

Silo passed it to her, and she took it, the smooth object in her hands. The weight was light, the black and white shell perforated. At one end was a piece of leather. Silo touched that piece, nodding with encouragement.

"This part I added myself."

"Ah," Agnes said in response.

There was silence once more, only the bleating of the child, whom Silo appeared to ignore as Agnes could not.

"It is for Godwin, so that you may feed him with further ease. See, here, it takes milk."

Agnes sucked in the air, wondering how she was meant to fill the horn from her breast. It was as tough as allowing the child to touch her to latch on. She thought then, as she held the nail-textured implement, that she might do whatever was required to stop from ever being touched again.

"We can use goats' milk," Silo said, as though Agnes had spoken aloud, or he could read her mind.

"We do not have a goat."

"Do we not?" Silo said, smiling. With care, he grasped Agnes' shoulders, directing her to the door, where beyond the wind that trickled into the house, beyond the waterwheel that creaked the heartbeat of their days, stood a small female goat. A string was tied about its neck.

"Oh," Agnes breathed, her gaze falling upon the udders that hung beneath the creature's legs. Was that how she looked, she wondered, hooves splayed and eyes staring?

"I thought that you would be pleased, for Finn says that Saskia finds it much to her benefit. She is able to leave the child with others for small periods of time, to visit the tavern or her mother."

Agnes listened. A strange thought, to leave Godwin. She longed for it, but feared it. Longed to be alone, to hear nothing but the trees whispering about her, feel no eyes upon her but those who could not speak a human language.

"Thank you, Husband. I do believe it shall be of great help."

Silo strode out with pride, milking the goat into a bucket quickly, as if it were a task that he had performed many times. As he did so, the goat bleated, her sounds matching Godwin in tone and rhythm until Agnes could no longer tell from which being the sound came.

Then, Silo filled the horn, holding it in one hand as he scooped Godwin up in the other. The ease with which he did this was hard to endure, seeming to Agnes to be much easier than she ever found it. She watched as the child latched onto the leather, sucking small mouthfuls of milk through the contraption. There they stood, and Agnes found herself backing away silently, trying to remove herself from the kitchen. It was clear that they would survive without her.

*

Godwin's blessing was set for Sunday. There was nothing to be done about it: Agnes had tried.

"Surely, he has been blessed; the Grothi and the Widow Pluck came to the house especially," she said to Silo the evening before.

"He is to be blessed before the people, you know this. What sort of parents would we be if he were not blessed for the people? Take a moment, Agnes, and rethink your situation. You have taken him to market now, and he was fine. A public blessing is an honour–" Silo paused, raising his eyebrows as though he were underlining his thoughts, "that not everyone receives."

This was true, and Agnes knew it. Why they would be honoured, though, she could not determine. They were a poor family, though she supposed respectable in their way. Agnes looked around the winter kitchen, the dim glow from the candlelight and hearth revealing the dirt floor and seemingly endless skins.

"Why us, then?" she whispered into the room, causing Silo to turn on her with an intensity she hadn't felt since Godwin was born.

"Because we pay our tithes, Agnes. Because you bore a son for the tanner, meaning that the town of Locklear will have a tanner for years to come. Because I married a child of spring, however useless her gift may be, and showed my commitment to the community by doing so. Your rejection of such an honour embarrasses all of us, do you understand?" Silo's gaze was clear and still, a static river of rage waiting to burst forth. Agnes looked into him and saw the threat, felt the tingling on the back of her neck.

"You are right, Silo, my apologies. You have always paid our tithes, and I am grateful to be inside the family." The quiet words sprang into the air and did their magic, weaving calm and healing the situation.

Silo paused, listening as though the sentence was being repeated.

"You are a good mother, Agnes," he said, the first compliment he had ever given her. Agnes nodded, accepting it, her eyes drifting to Godwin thoughtlessly. It was a lie, of course, she thought. Some strange ruse to get her out of the house and into the church. This much she knew, and yet, she felt her cheeks flush all the same.

*

The Grothi was waiting at the front of the church as usual, and the Widow Pluck still by his side, as if she had moved permanently to Locklear. Beside them stood the season's talisman, proud and blossoming, her baby daughter held to her hip. Agnes saw Saskia's face sharpen as she entered with Godwin, watched her lean over and murmur something to the Widow, who in turn focused her gaze.

"Come in all, come and know the Gods," the Grothi called as the people filtered in, taking their pews. One of the wives hustled up the middle aisle and took Agnes' arm firmly, leading her up to the front. Agnes breathed out when she saw some other mothers sitting there, waiting for their blessing. Perhaps they weren't so special after all, weren't being singled out by the Grothi and his followers.

"Today is a blessing before the town and the Gods. Come to the front, children of Locklear and know your worth."

Alongside the rest of the women, Agnes stepped forward, holding Godwin firmly against her chest, his face hidden. With a tight smile, Saskia stood beside her, the scent of honey clinging and sticking to everything within her reach.

"Our talisman joins us this morning for the blessing of her daughter, Ethelfleda. Turn the children to face the front, and we shall begin the blessing."

Agnes breathed out, turning Godwin so that his face was not shown to Saskia. He faced the front now, his back against her, and Agnes felt his desire to move his head to glance beside him, the draw of Saskia's scent too strong. The Grothi moved down the aisle of women and babies with speed, muttering beneath his breath. After him strode the Widow Pluck, her silent watch making its way from each pair to the next. When they arrived at Agnes and Godwin, they paused and stepped back slightly. The Grothi took in the scene before him, looking at both the children's faces, and then lifted his eyes to Agnes.

"These children look uncommonly alike," he said plainly. Agnes felt Saskia shift beside her; she wanted to look at her face to see what she was doing, thinking, feeling. What was the answer to such a statement? It was unclear. Agnes said nothing, for what could be said? She bowed her head, indicating that she was ready for the blessing.

"For our Gods above us, may you bless this child Godwin, and remove it from the sins of its mother," the Grothi whispered, barely audible, his hand hovering over Godwin's head. He then moved forward so that his hot, sour breath was beside Agnes' ear and said, even more quietly, "If there is any kind of witchcraft here, you will be found out."

Godwin let out a great cry, filling the church with noise. Beneath her breast, Agnes' heart thudded.

Chapter Thirty-Four

As the weeks folded into months, Godwin grew. His limbs stretched daily, the clothes that Agnes had been given by various people in town no longer fitting him, with plenty of mending and making do. She kept him inside as much as possible despite the sun starting to lift its head above the frost.

The worst of it was that the child didn't smile. Agnes now knew he should be smiling and engaging with her at this age, for Finn had told Silo, who in turn had passed the information onto Agnes. Even when she placed him in front of her, desperate to get him to behave as Silo said the other women's babies did, he would cry. Agnes would make eye contact, cluck and purr, trying everything Silo had suggested, heard from various visits to the tavern. The child just watched her move about the house as though bored with the sight of her, squawking and vying for any attention but hers.

"So, you will take him to the women's group today, Agnes."

She jumped, not realising that anyone was in the room besides herself and Godwin. Agnes could almost see the words from Silo appear, dimpling the wooden table. Silo sat, watching her, his breakfast cooling. Beside him, Pa stared.

"I would rather—"

"Listen to your husband, damn you, child!" Pa suddenly yelled, causing Godwin to wake and howl into the kitchen space, his cry filtering up into the eaves to join the smoke from the fire.

Agnes felt a rage that matched the baby's. It began at the base of her stomach, stretching high into her throat, bulging in her neck. She felt it before she could try to make a noise this time. She knew the feeling. She was unable to speak, unable to respond. With a quiet pause, Agnes simply nodded, no longer fighting her tongue.

"Insolence is the cause of a great many arguments," Silo said, his words sharp. Slowly, they finished their meals, both men standing and leaving the kitchen for work without another sound. Agnes looked at her full dish of oats and picked up her spoon.

"Who is it that holds my tongue in such a way?" she asked aloud, trying to listen over the whimpers of Godwin.

After a moment, a dim response shuddered before her.

"It is your mother-in-law."

*

The women's group had already begun by the time Agnes arrived. As she walked up to the large door of Saskia's stone house, she shifted the basket onto her other hip, pausing. Hundreds of nails were hammered into the front of the door, each a small moment apart from the other. Agnes reached her hand up to touch one, curious. Nails were hard to come by, Agnes knew. Her father made some occasionally, but strangely, it was only ever to ship out to the kingdom. The people of Locklear wouldn't spend money on something that they could make do without. This display was almost shocking in its opulence.

The door opened without warning, Saskia's maid smiling politely at Agnes. When she stepped inside, she was surprised by the sudden change in temperature in the air. Although the weather outside was still bitter, frost dancing across leaves, Saskia's house was filled with warm mirages. The air, of course, smelled like honey, and Agnes glanced down at Godwin, whose eyes shone at the scent.

She hadn't wanted to come. She had paused and wept and considered lying, but then, Silo had returned in a burst. He had come to check on her. There was something in the back of her mind, her own voice, that told her if she did not force herself out, the consequences would be much worse.

"The ladies are through in the other room. May I take your cloak?" the maid asked, holding her hands out expectantly. Agnes shook her head, clutching the basket in her hand. With a small curtsey, the maid walked away up the hallway, humming. Agnes listened until she heard the noise move through to the kitchen.

Steadily, she too continued up the hallway and paused before the closed door, the voices of the women and the occasional squeak of a child dancing through the wood.

"She never shows up, does she, Saskia? Well, what does her husband say?" Agnes heard the voice and felt her heart catch in her chest. They were talking about her, undoubtedly.

"Oh, I don't know. He says she is struggling with motherhood, Finn says. In some ways, it's a shame, of course, but in other ways... well, has anyone seen her child? I'm not one to spread rumours, you know that, but–" Saskia's voice fell to a hushed whisper, and try as Agnes might, she could only catch one word. It was 'class'. She frowned, unsure of what could have been said.

"Ma'am, go right in." The maid was suddenly there again, having sidled up to Agnes noiselessly. Agnes heard a sharp intake of collective breath before the door opened. Saskia stood, smiling baby on hip. Her expression was one of surprise threaded with curiosity, and she stepped back and glanced around at the other women. Agnes looked about the room, seeing faces from church, their babies and toddlers playing in the middle. There was a discernible wrinkle of noses.

"Agnes. You came," Saskia said, taking her seat once more. With a murmur of agreement, Agnes walked in and sat at an empty stool, keeping her cloak folded about her. Silence descended. Agnes cleared her throat and looked down at Godwin, who let out a laugh of joy. It was the first time she had ever heard him make such a noise.

"Oh goodness, is this your son? He is joyful!" one of the women exclaimed, swooping forward and bending down to pluck the baby from his basket. Agnes tried to resist, but found herself frozen still, set by the gaze of Saskia.

"This is Agnes' son, Godwin," Saskia said slowly, watching the baby be lifted. Godwin laughed again as if this was all so normal, all so delightful.

"He is a sweet thing, Agnes. Look at that smile!" The woman who held him rested him on her hip so that he could look around the room. "I am Fortunia. I married last year. Perhaps you remember me from the Spring Feast? That sweetheart is mine." Fortunia nodded towards a young girl, who looked around eight months old, sitting in the middle of the room. She was wearing a neat dress, her sparse hair plaited. Agnes realised that all the children in the room were dressed as if for church. As though reading her mind, Fortunia turned her attention back to Godwin and grasped the worn woollen blanket that covered him between finger and thumb.

"He is growing fast, I assume? Hard to keep up, isn't it? Still, a change of clothes will keep that stench at bay."

"Oh, Fortunia, Agnes is the tanner's wife. We are each of us blessed with a position, and there's not much that can be done about it!" Saskia chuckled, the sound dripping with glee. "Come, let us swap children, Fortunia. You take mine, and I'll hold–"

Agnes leapt to her feet, swiftly taking Godwin from the arms of Fortunia and wrapping her woollen blanket about him. "No, no," she said, finding her voice, "he gets ever so cold."

Saskia's face quietened, becoming still. She nodded, giving a gentle kiss to her daughter. "Well, as you wish. Tell me, Agnes, who was it that helped deliver your child? After all, I know that the Grothi and the Widow Pluck were busy with me. The Gods bless us so, and it's hard to imagine the fate of two babies being born on the same day in such a small town, isn't it?"

The other women glanced at Agnes, who swallowed. "I had the help of the Widow Sewall," she said, looking to Godwin. Now facing her, he was no longer smiling. His nostrils flared and fluttered as if searching for a scent he couldn't quite reach.

"The...the Widow Sewall?" Fortunia whispered, her eyes flitting to Saskia's and back again. "Oh, Agnes, you have surely heard the rumours?"

Agnes felt the words coming as she had done in her kitchen earlier. They were inevitable. They were already in existence.

"She is a witch."

Godwin began to cry, his yell both hesitant and assured, as though he were making a point. Saskia tutted, standing before Agnes could register her movements, and swept Godwin from her arms, now with a child on each hip. In an instant, Godwin stopped crying. He stared at the clear and clean skin of Saskia and smiled widely, his gummy mouth stretched into a grin.

"There, he is entertained. They need entertaining, Agnes, you cannot expect him to sleep all day," Fortunia said busily, as if she had been asked for her opinion. Agnes nodded. Had she known that the child needed entertainment? She didn't think she had, though now it seemed so obvious.

"Witchborne," Saskia said, looking at Godwin plainly. "And he looks nothing like his father...or his mother." Her eyes flicked back to Agnes.

"So what? Does your daughter look like you or Finn?" Agnes spat, her words coming out harsher than she meant them to. She wanted to say more, to ask whether she was alone in feeling barely a thing for her own child. Was it possible that Saskia felt the same, that she knew about the lack?

"Well, now hold on a moment–" One of the other women who had only previously nodded at Agnes now stood, making her way over to Saskia and the children. "The Widow Sewall has some rumours to her name, but she isn't necessarily a witch. And anyway, Agnes is right, and not all babies are little versions of their parents." She stroked the cheeks of both Godwin and Ethelfleda and then paused, glancing between the two. "But my word..." she said beneath her breath, "these children are so alike. Fortunia, do you see this? Their eyes, nose, hair. They are little siblings!"

Agnes felt bile begin to rise again and swallowed it down, hastily standing and grabbing Godwin from the arms of the women. "They are just similar in age, that's all," she hissed, before making her way out of the room. As she left, she heard Fortunia let out a strange noise, and then say, "You don't think she bedded Finn, do you, Saskia?"

Raucous laughter followed, Saskia's own high-pitched trill clearly absent.

Chapter Thirty-Five

The child needs entertainment. The words floated around Agnes' mind as Godwin lay glumly before her, another weekday alone. He stared at her, silent. When she looked at him, really looked, she fancied that she could see the same shaped eyes as her brother once had. Her brother, whose face she had almost forgotten. Was that true, or was it simply a strange coincidence, a wish that the boy was her own? Agnes selected a turnip from the table and held it up to show Godwin, watching his eyes travel to it with mild interest. Perhaps it might have been true if she had wished that the child was her own, but as it was, Agnes couldn't see what difference that would make to her. She had her son, and her parents had still disowned her. She had her son, and her husband still viewed her with quiet disdain, the joy of Godwin's arrival now dissipated to normality. She had her son, and she was still alone.

Godwin reached out and took the turnip from her hands, lifting it to his mouth. Though it was uncooked, she let him explore it for a moment with his tongue, the way a puppy might. The fire crackled beside them, its scent filtering through the room. With a sigh, Agnes reached into the flames and selected a piece of white coal with fire still glistening on its surface. She rolled it across her skin, taking small pleasure in the lack of burns, though used to it. A noise caused her to glance up at Godwin, who was staring at the coal with fascination, the turnip forgotten.

"This is fire, Godwin," Agnes said, and she saw his eyes light up before her. Was it the fire, or that she was using words? She rarely opened her mouth to speak when it was just the two of them, the one-sided conversation seeming pointless. But now, she saw a rare opportunity to share the gift that she had long kept hidden.

"I can touch fire without it burning me. That is my spring

blessing. Other people have all sorts of blessings, but that one is mine. I'm not allowed to tell anyone because it is so different from the other blessings. Do you understand?" Agnes said, watching Godwin narrow and widen his eyes as he listened. He made no more movement.

"If I told anyone else, I might get in trouble. Just like with you. If I told anyone about you and why I think you're really here, I might get in trouble." Agnes' voice stuck in her throat, saying the words aloud in her own kitchen, hurting the skin within. Tears threatened the backs of her eyes. Godwin looked from the coal to Agnes with some curiosity, and Agnes smiled.

"We'll be well, won't we?" she offered. Godwin looked blankly at her. She thought of Saskia, of how he had looked at her, his face breaking into a smile. It was a side she had never seen of him, not once.

"You are not a spring child, so you won't receive a blessing of this sort," Agnes said, continuing the conversation with herself.

"That is true," a voice said, and Agnes stared at the baby, watching his mouth to see if he had spoken. He hadn't. Slowly, she turned. There, in the doorway, stood Pa. With haste, Agnes threw the coal back into the fire, standing up.

"Pa, I did not realise you had come home. How long have you been there?" Agnes asked, her voice coming out cracked. Her tongue began to feel like lead in her mouth, chalky and dry.

"But a moment. You are telling Godwin about spring blessings, I see." Pa stepped in and closed the door behind him, walking to and sitting at the table. His gait was, even though he didn't speak, loud and voluminous. It was as though his very existence created noise.

Agnes nodded. "Yes. Can I get you a cup of soup, Pa?"

"You cannot. Why are you telling the boy about spring blessings?"

The air tingled in anticipation. Agnes cleared her throat to see if sh could, curious. "Because it is the culture of Locklear."

"It is the culture of the entire land, Agnes. Have you never stepped outside of the boundaries?" Pa began to remove his boots laboriously, one at a time.

"I have not." Of course, Agnes thought, she had not. Few had.

"It is a land filled with the same blessings as Locklear," he said, staring straight at Agnes. "Rumours abound. Are you aware of them?"

Her mind first fell to the memory of the Widow Sewall telling her about her mother-in-law, and Agnes' eyes glanced up to the rafters. There was nothing there, but Agnes fancied she could see a rope, a swinging body, a neck stretched—

"Agnes," Pa said, pulling her back to the present. She shook her head, not in answer to her name, but in response to his question.

"The rumours are that you visited the Widow Sewall to do something untoward..." Pa sighed as if conversing with a wayward child. "Is there any truth to this rumour?"

Agnes sat down once more and looked at Pa across the table. He looked tired, old, but still strong. His hands were folded in front of him, and as she glanced at them, Agnes could envisage them wrapped around her neck. She shook her head, not even trying to speak. She knew, almost instinctively, that she wouldn't be able to make a sound.

"How many times will I have to sit at this table and have this conversation?" Pa said, his eyes resting on the fire. "The women who come into this house don't seem to be able to keep themselves on the side of the Gods. What is it about the Grothi's sermons that you do not understand, Agnes?"

Breathing out, Agnes found she was able to whisper. "I understand the Grothi's sermons. But there is nothing wrong with seeking help from a midwife."

Pa nodded, scratching his ear with a strange haste. Agnes watched pieces of skin flick off into the air, falling like snow.

"The Widow Sewall has a reputation. Perhaps these rumours are from nothing, I do not know. But I will say this. That boy," he jabbed a finger in the direction of Godwin, "looks nothing like you or my son. The people of the town are saying as much. Looks strange, doesn't it, Agnes? To visit a witch and come back with a child that doesn't resemble you at all."

Agnes said nothing. Godwin watched the moving mouth of his grandfather.

"I don't know how much you know about my late wife," Pa said suddenly. Agnes glanced up and saw a strange look in his eye. It wasn't regret, wasn't grief. It was as though he was simply remembering, rigid, emotionless.

"I know a little," Agnes whispered, her voice a strangled tremor.

"She was with child when she died. She visited the Widow Sewall also. You know, we don't have a great many midwives in this town, which is why the Widow Pluck visits us from afar. But what we do have is more options than most. We have the Widow Tideswell. She is an honest woman and an honest midwife, though costly. My wife is no longer with us, as you know."

Agnes sniffed, wanting to break free of the conversation, to yell what she already knew. But she said nothing, and Pa continued.

"What I am trying to tell you, Agnes, is that you have made the wrong decision. When we decided that Silo needed a wife, we went to Saskia. We did that because she was arguably the most eligible woman in Locklear, as was her mother before. But we weren't stupid, Agnes, we knew that our family was not of the same level as hers. We asked her for advice, and she mentioned you. And it was set. A blacksmith's daughter marrying a tanner, that makes sense. Your brother had left to fight against the kingdom. This meant that you would not say no to my son; how could you? Your reputation was precarious. I thought you knew that, mind. It seems you like to live life on the edge of respectability. But let me be clear: after you showed my family up at the Spring Feast, after you chose a witch to be your midwife...after you bore a child that is so unlike us that it is to be suspicious...if any of the rumours about you continue, are proven to be true—"

"I cannot help rumours about me," Agnes spat, her voice suddenly sharp and fresh. It was as though it was coming from a different place than usual, within her stomach.

Pa paused, clearly unused to being interrupted, and especially by a woman. His gaze hardened further, skin into ice.

"You will come out and denounce the Widow Sewall and all of this nonsense. You will state it publicly. I can set it up at the church, with the Grothi by your side. If you do not put an end to these rumours, the rumours will put an end to you. Do you hear me?"

Agnes did. The thought of denouncing the Widow Sewall sent a pang through her body, a hardened stick of regret. If she did that, the Widow would have every right to tell the truth. And then what? It would be one word against the other, the screams of woman against woman. It was woman's inhumanity to woman, and the idea was perhaps worse than admitting her errors.

Chapter Thirty-Six

Whispers abounded. Agnes felt them sting her ears like gnats, flitting around her mind as she stepped through town, Godwin held firmly against her chest. Her cloak was wrapped about him, their heartbeats a mismatched duet—hers steady, his quick and light. Did he know of what they spoke, like a dog sensing that something wasn't quite right with the world?

"Did you hear?" one voice murmured to another as she passed by the vegetable stand. She fixed her gaze ahead, forcing one foot in front of the other. *Eggs. Just eggs,* she reminded herself, clinging to the simplicity of her errand.

The poultry farmer's wife stood sentry at her stall, arms crossed, eyes cold as river stones. "What do you want?" she asked, voice barbed.

"A dozen eggs, please," Agnes said, her breath dancing before her in the cold air.

"Perhaps I don't have any to sell," the woman responded, her tongue moving inside her top lip, as if trying to dislodge the remnants of food. Agnes looked at the display before her. There must have been fifty eggs. She cleared her throat.

"I can see that there are eggs for sale at your stall, ma'am, and simply wish to purchase some for my family," Agnes said, keeping her voice level. She was determined to leave with what she came for.

"You're the tanner's wife, aren't you?"

Agnes nodded.

"I've heard all about you. What was it you said to the Widow to get her to help you in such a treacherous way? It's not born of the Gods, and from a spring child too." The woman shook her head, her disgust clear.

"I...I am simply trying to buy eggs for my family."

A shrill noise travelled through the air, and the woman glanced beyond Agnes, her eyes creasing into a smile. Agnes turned, seeing Saskia bounding over, her child wearing its own small woollen clothes and resting on her hip. Saskia had her teeth bared, a wolf ready for the kill.

"You're not sold out of eggs, a blessing indeed, Mrs Shift!" Saskia trilled, glancing at Agnes briefly.

"Oh, I would have had the chickens make more for you, miss, given that you're our talisman!" the woman responded, her countenance entirely changing.

"Saskia," Agnes began, holding Godwin firmer still. She watched her honey-coloured eyes travel from her face to the back of Godwin's head and gave a tight smile.

"Agnes. There are some terrible rumours going around about you. Are you aware?"

Agnes nodded silently.

"Still, Finn tells me that you are to set it all right on Sunday at church. The Grothi is ready. Are you buying eggs?"

"I am trying," she said, flicking her gaze back to Mrs Shift.

"Mrs Shift, rumours are rumours. It is true that our children look...uncommonly alike. But Agnes will clear all of this up in front of the Gods on Sunday. And as you know, the Gods are not forgiving of sinners. If she has done wrong, let it be decided by them alone."

Agnes frowned, confused by Saskia's words. Was she being kind or trying to get her to confess?

"The Gods blessed me with both my Spring Gift and with Godwin. If the Gods see all, then they would have seen how he was conceived," Agnes said clearly. The words were true, surely. If the Gods saw all, then they knew exactly what was going on. And yet, they had done nothing to stop it.

Mrs Shift picked up half a dozen eggs and passed them slowly to Agnes, who took them gratefully. Saskia gave her a look of interest.

"Well, we shall find out what is what on Sunday, shan't we? Good day." Her child gurgled on her hip, a smile spreading. The dimples that alighted the baby's cheeks were uncommonly familiar. When Godwin cried, he, too, had dimples, as if his face were trying to force him into a smile.

Agnes handed over the money to Mrs Shift and turned smartly, holding both the eggs and Godwin close to her. For a moment, she found herself wondering which she had more connection to, the eggs that she would take home, cook and eat, or the child that clung to her for the lack of anyone else. Her heart couldn't decide.

Chapter Thirty-Seven

Pa had barely said a word to Agnes since their discussion, and Silo had been quiet himself, though he greeted Godwin with the dawn and kissed him gently on the forehead before bed. Agnes observed these rituals through a gauzy veil as if witnessing scenes from someone else's life. Their home had transformed into a stage, each family member an actor in an unsettling play, like they sometimes had at the Spring Feast, all desperately maintaining the illusion of normalcy while truth lurked in the wings.

Sunday loomed on the horizon, its approach relentless and suffocating. As a knock echoed through the house, Agnes knew it wasn't Silo returning from the workshop, nor Pa at his own threshold. Godwin, who was lying beside the fire upon a blanket, staring into the flame, glanced up at his mother at the sound, sensing what this meant. Agnes knew, too.

With a hesitant step, she moved towards the frame and pulled back the wood. There stood the Widow Sewall, her cloak pulled low. She didn't wait for an invitation, just stepped swiftly inside the door and closed it behind her, before pulling down her hood and taking a seat.

"Rumours abound, Agnes," the Widow murmured, her eyes flickering briefly to Godwin, before fixing on Agnes with unsettling intensity.

"Yes, I am aware." Agnes took a seat opposite her, not offering any hospitality.

"You are to forsake me tomorrow, I hear."

The Widow's words hung in the air, a challenge and an accusation intertwined.

Agnes cleared her throat. The decision had eluded her, slipping through her grasp like smoke whenever she tried to pin it down.

How could she choose? To denounce the Widow would be to admit to a crime she couldn't prove yet couldn't deny. Godwin's presence was testament enough to *something* extraordinary.

Her gaze drifted to the child. He was undeniably not of her blood, and yet...hadn't he emerged from her own body?

"Who do you hear this from?" Agnes asked, licking her lips.

"The words fall about my ears like snow. The market is riddled with your name, and for some reason, mine is now synonymous with it. What will you say?" The Widow sucked in her cheeks revealing high cheekbones, jutting out at sharp angles, indicative of a life survived on cabbage stew.

"I don't know. If they think I am guilty of witchcraft, they will..." Agnes' voice trailed off. Drag her to the woods, wrap a rope around her neck. Pull her up so that she swung from the branches, at one with the bark. Let her fall and give her to the earth. The Wife's Lament played through her mind, a story her mother had told her as a child. Waiting beneath the dirt for her lover, friends only bones.

"What would they do if you told them the truth? That I helped you with the conception of your child, as you asked. That I helped you give birth, without even the aid of a scroll, which is more than the Widow Pluck can do. You would denounce me for aiding you in your time of need? Had you not had the child, what would they have done to you?" The Widow sighed the words, as though tired of them as soon as they left her mouth. She had a fair argument, and it was one that Agnes lingered on. What position would she be in had she not had Godwin? Perhaps she would be with child now anyway, her own. Perhaps she would still be desperate, trying. Perhaps she would be hanging from the rafters, feet dangling above the kitchen table at which she now sat.

"Perhaps you would be hanging from the rafters, having taken after your mother-in-law," the Widow Sewall said, as though Agnes had been speaking aloud.

"If I choose to denounce you, it is to save the lives of myself and my child," Agnes said. The Widow rolled her eyes.

"Your life is worth more than mine? Why is that, Agnes?"

Agnes shook her head. Truthfully, she did not know. It wasn't that her life was worth more; of course it wasn't. It was that she valued it more. Was there anyone who didn't value their own life above another?

"I didn't say that. But should they ask you the same, I doubt you would not denounce my name."

The Widow sighed. "I have already passed that test, Agnes, many times. I have not, and would not, denounce you. You are just a child. You don't know the people in this village, and yet you strive to impress them, day after day. They are not your friends, those who whisper about you. The sooner you realise that there is no difference between what I do and what the Grothi does, the better. We all have gifts from the Gods, but we use them in different ways." The Widow reached out and touched Godwin's shoulder, who gazed back in response.

He let out a wail, a small plea that made Agnes jump. She pulled her cloak around her, noticing draughts in the room, the feeling but not the temperature unfurling around her skin.

"Did your mother tell you when you were a child, of the women who were witches in our town?"

Agnes thought back, stretching her mind to her childhood. Of course there were stories about witches, of course, the Grothi had said the words that they all came to expect. Witches were in the town and if you didn't watch where you were stepping, if you weren't careful to keep your blessings within the sights of the Gods, you risked attracting a witch. As Agnes had invariably done.

"Yes, she did, of course."

"Belief is a powerful thing. Sometimes, belief is the only thing. What do you think the difference is between the Widow Pluck and I?"

Agnes thought for a moment. The difference was, in fact, clear. The Widow Pluck had a solid reputation, a good midwife from out of town, who travelled to help the women of Locklear from the goodness of her heart. She was the chosen Widow of the Grothi. The Widow Sewall smiled, nodding.

"The Widow Pluck has the Grothi by her side. The people think she is holy. The Widow Pluck had children, you know, in her marriage. Eight of them. They all lived. Her husband died, and the children grew. I didn't marry, and I chose no child to grow within me. I *chose* not to follow that path, Agnes, and despite being born in this village and living here my entire life, I have never truly been accepted. But really, what the Widow Pluck and I do is very similar. Our path to the Gods is the same."

Agnes nodded. She had chosen this path despite the pressure. Perhaps she could have chosen another, like her brother, but she did not.

"I feel nothing towards him," she said with a burst, allowing the thoughts she had hidden away to lurch from her lips. "There is a lack of…feeling."

The Widow Sewall nodded, her expression not changing. "And so it is for many women."

"Not so for the women that I see with children around me, Widow Sewall. Not so for them."

The two paused, watching each other for a moment. The Widow Sewall then reached out a hand and lightly touched Agnes with it before withdrawing again. Godwin waited, silent.

"You are a mother, Agnes. But it is not a mother who makes a woman. You are a woman, but it is not a woman who makes a mother. He will be quite well. As for you and I, we must wonder."

A creak on the stairs made Agnes flit around, and she stared, seeing no one there. Her heart began to rattle in her chest. "If Pa sees you here, we will both be done for. Do you understand?"

The Widow Sewall smiled, standing slowly, the joints in her limbs seemingly stalling her movement. "Oh, I understand. It was the same with your mother-in-law, of course. She watches you, as no doubt you're aware. Though there's nothing she can do for you now."

With that, the Widow left the house, closing the door behind her. Agnes stared at Godwin. *And so it was for many women*, the Widow Sewall had said, as though the lack was displayed by more mothers than herself.

"You will be quite well, Godwin," Agnes whispered. As for herself...she wondered.

Chapter Thirty-Eight

The procession to the church was slow and steady, Agnes holding Godwin as her only protection. It felt that way, with Pa and Silo stepping ahead, their gaits quicker. Would the Widow Sewall be there? Agnes had never seen her in church. There was a whisper of spring in the air, and Agnes' mind found an image of herself a year ago, innocent and unsuspecting.

Saskia was standing by the door as she approached, a small smug smile on her face, her daughter in her arms. When she made eye contact with Agnes, she bowed her head slightly and sighed, whispering when she came close.

"You are doing the right thing, Agnes. The behaviour of witches in this town cannot be just left to the Gods to deal with. We must be the messengers; we must stand tall against them. Whatever she made you do was surely not your fault."

Agnes pulled back, gazing into the woman's eyes. It was her own fault, and she knew it. She was the one who had gone to the Widow Sewall, she was the one who had suggested the idea, put the thought in the mind of the old woman. What right did she now have to stand in front of these people and proclaim her a witch?

Agnes brushed past her erstwhile childhood friend and kept walking behind Silo and Pa, into the church, where the congregation were taking their seats. A few of them peeked around excitedly, their faces pictures of lurid curiosity. They wanted blood. They wanted entertainment. Agnes looked down at Godwin, who stared into the distance, accepting his fate as her child. In a moment, she felt him being lifted from her arms and glanced up to see Silo taking him.

"You cannot go up there with him, Agnes," he whispered, his voice still. Then, he leaned in further and sighed. "Do the right thing. For me." His eyes met hers, and Agnes nodded. This was the first time he had spoken to her about it. His plea was clear: don't leave me with the child.

Agnes left the pair to take their pew and walked towards the front, where the Grothi was waiting. His robe today seemed brighter than usual, the whiteness almost blurring Agnes' vision. He gave her a look of contempt and then lifted a hand, causing the congregation to fall silent. How many women had Agnes seen pulled to the front of them all, to denounce behaviour as witchcraft? Not one. The judgement was usually handed out while the town slept, the decisions made by the Grothi. She had never seen nor heard it enacted in this way. It had surely happened, but where had she been? Agnes turned and looked out into the crowd and saw the unexpected. At the back of the room, her mother and father were sitting, gaze heavy. She made eye contact with her father and watched his glare soften. He blinked slowly. Agnes blinked back, as if it were a secret signal between the two of them.

"Before we begin our usual prayers today, before we allow ourselves to give up our weeks to the lords above, who watch us sin and apply for their forgiveness, we must first invite Agnes to the front. For those who may not know, though I perceive that number to be minimal, Agnes is here to discuss her child, Godwin," the Grothi said, his voice low. Agnes' heart began to beat quickly, hard in her chest, a rhythm of fear. The Grothi had paused, looking out into the seated crowd, as if he expected something to happen then. Agnes wondered whether she should leap into the air and shout for forgiveness. In reality, she had no idea what she should do. A baby cried somewhere in the room, but Agnes could tell it wasn't Godwin.

"Rumours are always present in a town," the Grothi continued, his pause unrecognised. "Rumours are stories that we tell others to keep our loved ones safe. If you hear that the bridge over the river beyond town has broken, do you not take the long route around the trees? The next time you hear a rumour, consider it to be the truth for a moment and wonder at how it shall keep you safe. We all know about the witchcraft through the land. The kingdom has long worked to keep us safe, and we can trust that those words from up high are not rumours." The Grothi moved slowly now, close to Agnes, and laid a hand on her shoulder. Agnes watched the congregation's eyes move with the hand, following the Grothi's movement.

"Agnes has lived in Locklear since she was born. She is the definition, perhaps, of a member of our society. She is married to our tanner. She is the daughter of our blacksmith. She is one of the Daughters of Spring. And yet, you see," his dull and heavy voice continued, his hand remaining, "she is standing before you today to clear up a *rumour* about her. Agnes has been accused, through the whispers of town, of being connected with witchcraft."

Despite everyone surely knowing where his speech was leading, a few people in the congregation gasped audibly. Agnes breathed in the stale air, focusing now on the doors at the back of the church, her mind heavy, her tongue flat in her mouth.

"Agnes, did you knowingly engage the services of the Widow Sewall to profit from evil? Did you ask the Widow to steal a child from a member of your community, to pretend the child is your own? Did you then deny that the swap had taken place, claiming that the child was your own?"

Agnes blinked, the questions coming too fast to answer one alone. She cleared her throat, trying to focus not on the congregation but on the images of the Gods at the back of the church. Surely, they would have an answer for her, a way forward. Their painted eyes stared out as they always had, not focusing, not gifting Agnes with any sense of completion. With a sharp breath inward, she opened her mouth to speak. The congregation leaned forward as if one body.

"I will not denounce the Widow Sewall, and I myself have done nothing but bear a child." The words fell into the air before her, and the witnesses leaned back once more. There were no other noises, save for a lonesome bird singing outside the church, its call an isolated focus.

The Grothi removed his hand from Agnes' shoulder and she turned to look at him. His face was sour, sharp.

"You will not denounce the witch that assisted you in your sin?" he said clearly.

Agnes shook her head. "There has been no sin. The Widow Sewall helped me birth my child, as a midwife. Her powers of healing are strong, as are the Widow Pluck's. The Widow Sewall was the midwife available to me on the day of my son's birth."

"Yes, because your son was conveniently born at the same time as our Talisman's daughter, as though twins in two wombs," the Grothi said. "You are aware that you speak before the Gods?" His left arm swept beyond the congregation, as though the people of Locklear were the Gods that he referred to.

"The Gods see all and know the truth of the matter," Agnes said calmly. She looked out and caught eyes with Silo, who had a curious look on his face. Whether it was disappointment or pleasure, Agnes could not tell.

"They do. And so there we are: Agnes has cleared up her part in this…situation. Though rarely is there smoke without fire, and I want to reassure the people of this village that I shall be questioning the Widow Sewall, too. As it is, without witnesses that something untoward has indeed happened, we must leave this rumour quelled. Agnes, take a seat with the other wives."

Agnes blinked in surprise, stepping off the stage and hurrying over to a pew, where the other wives avoided her desperate stares. So that was it? The rumours would end? As she sat back and tried to calm her beating heart, to moisten her dry tongue, Agnes wondered whether a new witness waited in the room. If there was, what would her punishment be?

SANGUIN SPRING

Chapter Thirty-Nine

Godwin was becoming more distanced. It was strange how he avoided Agnes' gaze, his eyes swivelling away from her whenever she moved close. He could hold his head up now and would seemingly strain his neck, always in one direction. Away.

Agnes pulled on her cloak and boots, lacing them tightly, knowing that spring's arrival would bring with it the mud.

"Godwin," she said clearly. He heard her, his body stopping still, listening. "We are to go to market." It was a day since their visit to church, and Agnes was determined to show her face, to show that she was not afraid of those who stalked the streets whispering her name. Despite the child's body stiffening, Agnes plucked him from the floor, balanced him on her hip, and left the house.

The market was busy, as ever, the sunlight whispering promises of warmer climes. The scents covered Agnes' face in a cloud of intrigue: spices and freshly baked bread, jams and sweet treats, cooked meats and smoked fish. Agnes took her time looking at the wares, noticing still the sharpness of the keepers. The people of the village invariably moved out of her way, a small path created ahead of her. When she reached the vegetable stand, Agnes smiled at the woman behind it, who pulled her apron tight.

"Three carrots and some of those turnips, please," Agnes said brightly, holding on firmly to Godwin, who was stretching towards the woman with his arms flung forward.

"You can pay?" she said in response, eyes glancing at the reaching baby.

"Of course."

With a hesitant hand, the woman began to select the items and, without care, dropped them in the basket Agnes carried.

"Thank you," Agnes said, attempting to reach into her cloak but struggling with the ever-squirming child.

"Come, I shall take him," the woman said, and she did so gently, taking him from Agnes' arms and delivering to him a bright smile. Godwin laughed, his hands touching the woman's soft cheeks. "You are a bonnie lad. It's none of it your fault, you hear me?"

Arms now free, Agnes found the money and placed it on the stall before her, watching the scene. Her heart ached. What for? There was an anger there, a jealousy for all that Godwin was with other people, other women. The child knew what had happened and, even before he could formulate words, was threatening to out Agnes by his actions.

"None of what is his fault?" Agnes said, surprised at herself. She knew the answer, so why did she ask the question? There was something within her that pushed against this woman's brazen commentary on their life. The woman turned from Godwin and gave Agnes a slight smirk.

"Your meddling in witchcraft to bear a son. That's what."

Agnes' heart began to beat in her ears, and she pulled her

cloak tight around her, leaning forward. "Were you not at church yesterday?" she hissed.

The woman nodded. "I was indeed. And I heard nothing that would assuage my suspicion."

"Give me back my child."

The woman pushed Godwin back into Agnes' arms, and he began to squawk, his displeasure ear-bending. With her spare hand, Agnes took her basket.

"Watch your tongue," Agnes said sharply before turning away. The eyes of the people watched her step through the crowds, some whispering, others sighing, her presence an inconvenience.

As she made her way from the market to her home, she passed Saskia, who stood, conversing with another mother. They caught eyes, and Saskia gently shook her head, no polite smile forthcoming. For reasons Agnes could not discern, her stare made her truly afraid.

*

Two days had passed, and Agnes had stayed indoors, tending to the hearth and her small family alike. Time was repeating in such a way as to make her feel strange, as though every moment had been lived before, and as she pushed the stew that they were once more having for dinner over the fire, she allowed her eyes to close.

"Death."

Agnes flinched, the word seeping into her stilted tranquillity. She looked up from her pot, seeing Pa standing in the doorway, his frame silhouetted by the setting sun. His face was hard, stern, bare. It was as though he was staring at a mere stranger.

"What?" she asked, her tongue heavy in her mouth. What did he want, coming in and saying such things to her of an evening?

"Death. You have brought it to our household."

Agnes sighed, stirring a turnip back into the stew that bubbled before her. "I have brought life to the household, Pa. See that baby?

I gave birth to him right here. Birth, the opposite of death, or perhaps you are confused."

"You cursed the vegetable stall owner two days ago for saying she didn't believe you. The people saw it, heard it. They watched you leave, a curse upon your lips and Godwin on your hip."

Agnes paused, thinking desperately back to the interaction. She had told her to watch her tongue. But how could words curse a human in such a way? When she had visited the Widow Sewall, she had, at least, drunk something. She had done more than speak some thoughtless words, some simple chime of nothing. Agnes drew breath to speak but found her tongue catching again, as though swollen to fill her mouth.

"And so, you cannot deny it," Pa said. Agnes opened her mouth to make a noise but could not. She wanted to scream, to shout out all the things that she knew the man had done. He had killed his last wife, pregnant with child.

"You–" was all she managed, the word falling out of her mouth in a hollow hiss, a strange noise she could barely keep within.

"Well done, sir," a voice crept into the kitchen, and Pa stepped aside to reveal the Grothi. "You have done the best you can to get her to confess, but alas, there is no trusting the process on these occasions. Come, Widow Pluck, gather the child." Behind him, the Widow Pluck followed obediently, purposefully keeping her eyes on the ground, her gaze not shifting to Agnes. She picked up Godwin from his space on the floor and cooed gently to him, as though he were her own child. With a shiver, Agnes stared. She watched as the woman wrapped her cloak around him and stalked back out of the door. As though never leaden, Agnes' tongue leapt into life again, the weight gone.

"Wait, you cannot take my child!" she said sharply, the shock of her voice seemingly a surprise to all. She began to step forward, reaching out. What had she hoped for, that the widow might turn back and return Godwin to her arms? Silo appeared then, as if he had been there all along, and firmly stood beside her, grabbing her shoulders so she was held still.

"You cannot take my child," she said again, staring at her husband. He barely made eye contact with her. The Grothi sighed as if this entire thing were far from what he wanted.

"Agnes, you have spoken before the Gods and claimed that you did not have this child in the abhorrent way suggested, and yet, you put a curse on one of the people of Locklear. With her last words, the stallholder informed us of what you said. You are brazen, and we cannot have a child of the Gods within such a grasp. It is unholy. You are under investigation and house arrest."

Agnes breathed out, her eyes stinging. Unholy? It was nothing of the sort. Every gift she had been given was from the Gods, and they were none of them witchcraft. No curse had been placed on anyone, apart from, perhaps, herself. Silo squeezed her arms gently and leaned forward. The space within her began to long, strangely, for the shape of the boy, Godwin.

"Agnes, you have killed a woman with your tongue. Do you understand? We cannot allow a child to be brought up beside you. Not my child. Godwin will go to a—"

"Where will he go?" Agnes shouted. Her throat was raw, pulsating, as if a heart was hidden within it.

The Grothi stepped forward and raised his hand, palm flattened towards the roof of the building. "He will go to the village and will become the property of Locklear. He will be supported by our people, grow as a trustworthy member of the church. Your husband has agreed to keep you for tonight while we source a carer. You are not to leave this house."

With that, as though all questions were answered, all worries quelled, he turned. Agnes watched as the people left her house, one after the other, Pa included. The door locked from the outside, the sound of a piece of wood being slid across it clear. Silo stayed behind, his face bare.

"I will see him."

"And now what? I am only eighteen. We will do what, exactly?

You and I? Where are they going? They will not take me now, the witch?"

Silo stared at her as if he were looking at her skin for the first time, inspecting her. He said nothing.

"We will rot. In this house, with your father, a murderer. We will sit and stare and resent each other. Do you think that if I have another child, they will not take them? What sort of church does this?"

"What sort of woman visits a witch and asks for a child in the way you did?" Silo shouted, his voice rising through the hot air. Agnes flinched.

"You don't know that I did that," she murmured.

"I do. I do know, Agnes. Everyone knows. The Widow Sewall may as well have painted it on the door of her house. When they asked her, she all but admitted it. And now, you have cursed another."

Agnes breathed in, anger flaring. "If this is so, are you not afraid? Afraid to be standing before me, a witch?"

"You have cursed me already," Silo spat.

"And the Widow Sewall? If she is a witch, why has she not been dragged into the woods?"

"Her time is coming. And you forget, she is one of the few trained in midwifery in this town. If you think that your life is more valuable than hers—" He stopped mid-sentence, eyes hard. With one last short breath, he headed towards the stairs. Agnes watched as he bolted up them. Her heart thudded in her chest. Had the Widow Sewall all but admitted her faults?

In silence, Agnes left the pot cooking on the dying fire. She said nothing more, though her tongue was free enough for it. She waited beside the fire for around two hours, wondering if anyone would return to bind her arms. When they did not, she walked up the wooden staircase and folded her broken self into bed beside her husband. He breathed as though he slept. As she drifted off, she listened out for the cry of Godwin. It was not there, or if it was, it was so far from her ears that she could not hear it. Her arms ached with the lack of him. How strange to wish for that which she had never been sure was her own.

Chapter Forty

Agnes jolted awake, her body already upright, before her mind fully surfaced. The space beside her gaped empty—Silo was gone. An unnatural silence pressed against the window, as if the night itself held its breath. She strained her ears, seeking familiar sounds: Godwin's cry, Pa's murmur. But those had been taken from her.

"Agnes."

The voice, again. It felt as though it had been weeks since Agnes had last heard it, shattering into her brain. She pulled back the threadbare blankets and carefully lit the candle beside her bed.

"Flame," the voice insisted. Agnes sighed, eyeing the flickering light. Yes, it was flame—did it need narration? Her thoughts drifted to the Widow Sewall. Was she waiting, fear gnawing at her edges, dreading a fate in the woods? Agnes remembered the nighttime cries from her girlhood. Was that her destination now?

"Flame," the voice repeated, more insistent.

Agnes shivered, pulling her cloak around her, and then paused. A new sound pierced the silence—a high, keening whine, like a kitten bereft of its mother. She lifted the candle, its feeble light revealing little. Yet, as her eyes adjusted, she noticed an alien glow, pinching its way under the door, creeping along the wooden floor. Agnes followed its tendrils, tracing the brightness between the cracks in the floorboards. Beneath her feet, the world was bright. The light crawled through into the room, and it took Agnes a moment to realise what it was.

Flame. Fire. The voice had been trying to warn her. She could feel nothing of its heat.

"Pa!" Agnes ran forward, throwing the candle to the ground, and pushed her way into Pa's room. The floorboards there were already bitten by the flames beneath, and Agnes ran towards the bed. It, too, was empty. Both of the men had gone, had left her. They had left her to be engulfed.

Agnes began to cough. As smoke filled her lungs, a cruel irony struck her: a woman protected from fire, fated to suffocate in its embrace. She pressed her cloak to her mouth, forcing herself to take shallow breaths. The stairs, her only escape, had already been partly devoured. Agnes stepped onto the remaining treads, feeling them groan and splinter beneath her weight.

Agnes let her bare feet drop down onto the top few steps and felt them wane beneath her before they splintered and cracked in an almighty crash. The world twisted. She fell, her legs feeling heavy and bloated, and for a moment, a split second of infinite calm, time stopped. Agnes felt as though she could look around at the kitchen that was bright with fire, the flame that had leapt from the hearth while mid-air. She wondered if this was her doing, if she had let a spark devour the house in this way. And then, the second was over.

Her body seared with pain. The flames lapped around her skin, and though she could not feel their touch, her wrist and ankle were throbbing from the hard landing. Agnes tried to suck in a breath and, feeling her lungs fill with smoke once more, coughed. She was going to die.

The fire, relentless in its hunger, tore at her cloak. Agnes groaned, pushing debris aside as she struggled to her feet. She was losing. The fire was so large that it had now reached the roof, and Agnes could hear the strange sound of the thatch being engulfed, a noise that suggested the air itself was crying. The flame continued lapping at her, and Agnes stepped forward, fighting her way through, past the kitchen that she had once worried about keeping clean, the hearth that she had swept, the place where she had held up a piece of coal for Godwin, talked to him of her gift. Over the fallen rafters that had once held the swinging dead weight of a woman.

Eventually, she reached the door, or what was left of it. With a push, Agnes got through, stepping into the night air. At the threshold, she removed her burning clothes, trying to hold her breath. Now free, she staggered forward past the flame.

Her gaze was clouded by smoke, her throat sore from the fiery blaze, but Agnes knew the layout of her home, and she followed the shape of the large waterwheel. She fell to her knees once there, pushing her hands into the stream, and picked up the water in a cupped motion. She splashed it onto her face, feeling the relief in her eyes almost instantly. It cooled them, washed off the charcoal, cleansed her of the charred air.

Rubbing the water clear, Agnes looked around her. There, in front of the house, was more flame. It took her a second to clear her thoughts and to really see what it was her eyes beheld. It was fire on the end of sticks. There, before her, stood the townspeople. They stared back at her, their eyes wide. Agnes stood, naked now, in front of them.

"What have you to do with this?" she said quietly, the words disappearing. The people gawped. Agnes couldn't make out their faces, as if they were one body, but instinctively she knew that her husband and his father were among them.

"What have you to do with this?" she said again, much louder this time, forcing timbre to come back to her voice.

"She survives the fire!" a voice called. "She does the impossible! She is a witch!"

"She is!" Another voice filtered through the air. And then, a different voice, a quieter one, a voice that had become all too familiar.

"Fire."

Chapter Forty-One

There was only one place that Agnes knew to go to, and she headed there directly, the cold night air breathing on her naked flesh. The townsfolk would follow her, she knew, but there would be a moment of time where they stood, shocked for having seen her, wondering what next to do, encouraging each other to step forward. The door was open, and through it, Agnes had imagined she would see where the Widow Sewall stood, silhouetted.

As Agnes neared, she realised that there was no such sight. Where the Widow should have been standing, lit by the dimming light of a candle, a broom stood against the door as if it had been propped up on purpose.

She lingered at the threshold, peering in. It seemed empty, no Widow Sewall. Once certain she was quite alone, Agnes entered and closed the door, locking it. She grasped a rough woollen blanket from the floor and fixed it about her body, though for who, she did not know. Noise began to filter into her consciousness. It was the sound of a crowd, of voices merged, howls and hoots like wolves and owls, strange high notes of glee colliding with rage. They had found her.

Agnes' eyes scanned the small room and fell upon a long stick with a hooked end. She knew what this must be for; her parent's home had owned one, too. She looked at the ceiling and saw the small, rectangular shape, no doubt to filter the smoke out of the room when the fire blazed brightly in winter. It was just large enough for her body, she fancied, though at a push.

Agnes pulled the stool that she had once sat upon beneath the trap door and climbed up. Her head hit the night sky, and she heard the clamour of voices beyond, pushing herself until she lay low on the single-storey thatched roof.

"Come out of there, witch! Come and deliver the demons that you harbour! We have your accomplice."

Agnes looked down at the hole, almost expecting the Widow to come after her, to climb through with her. They had the Widow Sewall and held her, most likely in the church. Her mind pulsated with thoughts of helping the Widow, of finding her, heading back into town. To do so would be certain death, she knew. She looked down to the cold ground beneath. The drop was not far, and the people remained on the other side of the small house, clambering to get in. She had this small chance.

Agnes wrapped the blanket around her tighter, letting herself silently drop to the ground. The crowd became louder, baying for blood. Agnes heard them break through the front door and moved as fast as she could, into the darkness of the beyond.

As she pounded through the trees, Agnes turned to catch sight of the smoke rising from the dot that Locklear had become. She paused. The way that it rose into the air was erratic, dark and harsh whites spluttering through the night sky. It occurred to her then that the smoke that rose from a hearth, from a purposeful flame, was quite different. It had an almost ordered movement, as if conspiring with the wind to stay in shape. Looking upon the smoke as it poured from her old house into the sky was like watching something else entirely. It was panic, bleeding across the clouds.

*

The air was thick with early morning frost, spring sharing its memories of winter. Agnes had been walking all night, until the birds began singing in the trees, and had walked on further, until their voices hushed and the light once more disappeared. Her bare feet must have been numb, as she could no longer feel the stones and sticks beneath. The blanket was torn. On she walked, watching the sun as it rose in the sky, breathing out visible air.

Was this better than death? With a wry thought, she murmured to herself that at least if they had burned her, she might have been warm at last. But even so, she knew this was not true. There would be no warmth for someone with her gift.

Where was she going then? Agnes had never wandered this far from town, had never dreamt of it. What lay beyond the borders of Locklear was a mystery. The woods that she walked through were finally beginning to clear a little, though, and the trees were becoming sparser.

As the sun rose further in the sky, playing with the leaves, Agnes thought she heard a sound. It was a noise she hadn't heard in a long time, a strange tinkling. It was coming from up ahead. Her breath caught in her throat, her desperation for food taking over her brain. Perhaps it was a hunting party, she thought; maybe they would be able to feed her, clothe her. She began to run forward, holding her blanket ever tighter around her. The tinkling became clearer as the trees dispersed, and there she saw them. Two little girls were playing before her, both dressed in fine clothes.

"Look!" one of them yelled upon seeing her, grabbing her sister close. "She is bare."

The other caught eyes with Agnes and laughed aloud, the sound beautiful to hear. "You are bare!" she exclaimed, and both of the girls dissolved into giggles. Their accents were unlike anything Agnes had ever heard, lilting and sing-song, much more joyful than the accents of Locklear.

"Perhaps you may fetch me something to wear? A bite to eat?" Agnes tried, smiling as warmly as she could.

"You sound strange," one of the girls said, "like those who come to fight."

Agnes paused, frowning. "Those who come to fight?"

The elder girl nodded, impatient now, wanting to get back to her playing. "Yes. Are you one of those? Did the kingdom take your clothes?"

Agnes shook her head. "Might you find me something to wear, child, or show me someone who could help?"

The girls fell silent, considering her for a moment, serious looks now flickering across their faces. The younger opened her mouth to speak but was nudged by the elder.

"We can take you to Mother. Father is dead."

With a nod, Agnes allowed them to lead her.

Chapter Forty-Two

The house was much the same as Agnes had been used to, threadbare, the dry tinder needed to start fires, minus the waterwheel synonymous with a tanner. The girls were silent now, and Agnes took in the town. It appeared to be a single high street, with crooked small houses and huts jostling for position in the spring air. There was no stone here, no impressive structures bursting with yellow flowers.

The door was open to the elements, and the girls danced inside, forgetting Agnes was there at all.

"Hail?" Her voice trickled into the space. The sound of the girls giggling answered her in the ether beyond. Agnes stepped in and breathed the scent of a sweet stew cooking in the fireplace, the soft crackling of wood a welcome.

"Goodness–" the word brought her back to reality, and Agnes smiled, raising her hand.

"Where have you come from?" the woman before her asked, curiosity colouring her face.

Agnes pulled her blanket around her naked flesh. "A town far from here," she replied. "I was robbed."

The woman frowned as though she didn't believe her words. "Of your clothes? A feasible thing. Come, we are nothing if not generous with what little we have."

The comment stung as if she were telling Agnes that they, too, had nothing.

"Wait by the fire, warm yourself."

With that, the woman disappeared into the background, where Agnes could still hear the girls playing. She stared at the flames. Of course, she could not warm herself—it was an impossible feat. Instead, she merely stood and looked around the small kitchen.

The table was laid as if for a meal, and as Agnes found herself reaching for the ladle and bowl, the woman re-entered.

"Oh! I am sorry, I haven't—"

"You haven't eaten, of course. You must change into this and join us for food."

Agnes' breath caught in her mouth, the air not moving further from her throat. Instead of speaking, she reached out, taking the pile of clothing from the woman's hands. It was soft, clean, wool, seemingly new. Agnes stared in wonder as the woman guided her to the back room, pulling a once luxurious curtain around her so that she could change.

As Agnes dressed, the clothes falling against her body, she smelled the sweetness of the wool. These were not the second-hand clothes of Locklear; they were even newer than Saskia's own items. Agnes wondered at the possibility of this. How could it be?

Once dressed, she went back into the kitchen and hesitantly smiled at the small family, who were now sitting about the table, bowls of stew steaming before them.

"I...thank you for your generosity, but these clothes are far too fine...for the likes of me."

The woman winked at her daughters, who giggled, and then looked back at Agnes.

"Not at all. You will see that they are just as fine as our own."

Agnes watched the smiles, confused. The wool was so soft against her skin, and the stew smelled so sweet, that for a moment, a mere second, she almost forgot that she had lost everything.

"I am grateful that you have helped me. What is your name?" Agnes asked, silently cursing her previous rudeness.

"Bess," the woman answered. "And this is Nyx and Fly. You'll find us a helpful bunch here." Her smile was warm, and Bess motioned to the bowl before Agnes, encouraging her to begin. Agnes did so without hesitation. She speared the meat floating in the thick broth and pushed it into her mouth, feeling the taste buds spring into action. It felt like forever ago that she was last sitting in a kitchen, eating stew.

"Where do you come from...?" Bess asked.

"Agnes. I...come from a village, about a day or so's travel away."

The girls glanced at each other and giggled, and Bess raised a hand, silencing them.

"Come, girls. Do you come from the kingdom, Agnes?"

Agnes shook her head in response. Bess stared at her for a moment, gaze steady. It was clear that she was searching her face, checking for the truth of the matter. When she was satisfied, she took a mouthful of her food.

"We wouldn't like you if you were from the kingdom," Nyx, the eldest child, said with a serious look on her face.

"Nyx, please. That is not true," Bess replied.

"It was those people from the kingdom that killed our father," Fly stated while chewing, which seemed like a strange, nonchalant act to accompany such a serious statement. Agnes found herself staring.

"Apologies, Agnes, but my daughter does not speak out of turn. We have had many lost to the battles with the kingdom, and we don't welcome trouble here. And yet...occasionally, it comes to us. Have you problems in your own town?" Bess asked.

Agnes shook her head and then caught herself, remembering the very reason she sat before the strangers, dressed in fine wool. "Not with the kingdom, no."

"Then you are lucky, perhaps."

"Perhaps," Agnes said, continuing to eat.

After the meal, Bess and her daughters cleared the table, refusing to let Agnes help. Swiftly, Bess put the children to bed for a nap and then pulled up a stool beside the already crackling fire, the still wintery sun going down outside behind her. She smiled at Agnes and cleared her throat.

"You are...blessed?" Bess began, leading the sentence to a curious lack of conclusion.

Agnes pulled her shawl about her for no reason other than habit and frowned. "What do you mean?"

"Well, the blessings of the Gods. What is it that you have received?"

"I can bring water from the lake to the house," Agnes said, the old lie.

"That is not a blessing; that is a chore."

There was silence for a moment, and Bess sighed. "I am blessed. A lot of women in our town are."

"You were born in the spring?"

Bess looked at Agnes strangely for this comment and shook her head. "The spring? No. I was born in the depths of winter."

"Oh. Where I come from...those who are born in the spring receive the blessings. Is it different here?"

"The Gods decide who are blessed, not the seasons. Some are born with strong blessings, others more subtle...and some with none."

Agnes watched the crackling of the fire and considered this. "Our Grothi blesses us. He is the path from the Gods."

Bess made a sound of acknowledgement and shrugged. "Our Grothi was chased out of town years ago for stealing the altar wine."

"And no replacement?" Agnes asked.

"What replacement should there be? We are perfectly capable of conversing with the Gods ourselves."

Were they? It was a new idea to Agnes, one she had not considered before. Agnes fingered the soft blanket-like material that covered her, the clothes that were so well made. "How come you by these clothes? They are beyond what we have in Locklear."

Bess smiled. "That's my blessing, Agnes. Blessings are always useful; it depends on how you wield them."

Agnes leaned forward, selecting a coal from the fire. She turned slowly, holding it up for Bess to see. Bess' face was clear, unsurprised, and she simply smiled and nodded.

"Wonderful, a great blessing."

"You are not afraid?" Agnes asked, the coal burning brightly.

"Afraid? Of what?" Bess asked, laughter in her voice.

"Of me…I hold fire, I feel nothing, it cannot burn me."

"Well, the Widow Shank down the road has the same blessing, and it is very useful."

Agnes felt her tongue expand in her mouth, the years of strangeness washing over her, lies upon lies, words upon words, rumours upon rumours.

Chapter Forty-Three

For three days, Agnes waited by the door inside Bess' home, certain that they were coming for her. She would flinch when one of the girls called her name and hesitate when Bess asked her to join her for a walk. On the fourth day, Bess joined her at her post and laid a hand on her arm.

"Agnes, you are always on the lookout. Are you certain that the robbers will find you here? They took all that you have. What more could they want?"

Agnes licked her lips, trying to find the words to explain her concern. She had reviewed her story numerous times over the days, but had not the strength to tell it.

"Bess, I do not fear the robbers, but I fear rumours and people from my old town."

Bess nodded, breath still.

"Do you intend to stay, Agnes, or will you travel on further?"

Silence settled. Agnes thought of the town she found herself in, of the differences between here and that which was once her home. Here, though she had mainly stayed within Bess' walls, hiding from view, women filled the streets. She had heard their voices calling to each other, bidding good morning, good afternoon, a blessed evening. She had listened to the girls playing outside with women of all ages, laughing and helping each other. For the first time, she had wanted to step outside and join in.

"What is there to call you back?" Bess asked, piercing the silence after Agnes' lack of response.

"There is nothing," Agnes said, thinking of the Widow Sewall, who may have been waiting inside a cell at that very moment.

"You have no family, then."

Agnes thought of her mother, her father, their faces blank and distant. She thought of Silo, his rage. She thought of Godwin, someone else's child. Finally, she thought of her brother. She shook her head.

"If that is the case, then you must stay. We can find you a home here, Agnes."

"I have no money." The words hung in the air.

"So you will find a job, and with your blessing, Matil, the blacksmith, might take you on as an apprentice."

Agnes laughed aloud, the suggestion so strange and wonderful that it couldn't be true.

*

Days passed, folding into weeks. Agnes often noticed a strange feeling in her arms, a different type of lack. It was the lack of Godwin. But, as time passed, her arms started to grow lighter, becoming used to the distance.

The weather changed, the seasons blessing the people with each gift. Bess, true to her word, took Agnes to the blacksmith, who accepted her as an apprentice, paying a fair wage. With care, Bess and her children helped Agnes find a very small dwelling, cleaned it, and made it soft and comfortable, softer than any home Agnes had ever had. At night, she slept alone, going over her life in detail. Every night, she asked herself the same question: what might she have changed?

The rugged truth was that there was no turning back time. But something was holding her back from giving herself over to this life. When Bess introduced her to people, she found herself fretting, her gaze flicking over their features, trying to find any suspicion in their eyes. There was none, but her lack of truth with Bess was holding her back, and this she knew.

On the twenty-ninth day since her arrival, Agnes knocked at Bess' door in the early morning. Bess opened, yawning, and welcomed Agnes in. Before she could say a word, Agnes began.

"I stole a child from another woman's stomach. I had it in my own, Bess," she blustered out clumsily. "I went to the Widow Sewall, and she helped me do such a thing. I took a woman's twin, I took a baby and grew it as my own..." The words shuddered and slipped out of Agnes' mouth, and she began to sob. She cried for the first time since it all began, since she had lain alone in bed, waiting to marry the tanner's son.

"Agnes," Bess said softly, "it is not possible."

"But the child, he was not my own." Agnes heaved out the words, telling Bess the tale from start to finish. In silence, Bess listened, eyes wide.

Once Agnes was finished, Bess carefully made a drink at the stove, her silence a comfort rather than a judgment. After a while, she turned and placed a cup in Agnes' hand, joining her by the hearth.

"Agnes, the world is full of all sorts of people: those afraid, those brave, those willing to put another at risk for their own benefit. But here is the truth as I see it. The Gods do not play with lives in the way that you describe. You may never know whether the child was your own or not, but you can know this: he is safe, as are you."

With that, Bess patted Agnes on the hand and gently wrapped a blanket around her shoulders. With a kind smile, she went to wake her daughters.

Agnes sat for a while, staring at the dying fire and closed her eyes, feeling the softness of the clothing once more. She let herself drift off into sleep, her arms cradling the air. Her ears no longer listened when she tried to rest, no longer strained to hear the baby cry. Belief was a powerful thing indeed.

*

"Agnes!"

The voice swam to her, clear and sharp. Agnes felt for her

throat before opening her eyes, certain that the next breath she took would be stilted and trapped, her tongue so swollen that she could not speak. But it was not so. The voice was real. Agnes breathed out slowly, opening her eyes to look upon Bess.

"Agnes," she said again, as though her voice had not travelled before. "News from the kingdom."

Agnes sat forward slowly, without hurry. She was still sitting before the fire inside Bess' home, the day now later. News from the kingdom? Her mind moved backwards to the Grothi, standing in front of his people, delivering his sermons with murmurings of the kingdom, their safety, and the gracious royalty bestowed upon them.

"They have won the war. Agnes, they have slaughtered all who stood against them."

Agnes stared into Bess' eyes and felt a strange feeling move across her skin, plucking at the pores. Was this what people felt when they grew cold?

"How do you know? How can they have—" and then, a face flashed into her mind. She stood in haste, raising her hand to her head. "My brother."

Bess stepped backwards, her head leaning onto one side, curious. "I thought that you had no family?"

"I did have, once. My brother left us to fight against the kingdom, and—Bess, will this news have travelled to other towns?"

Bess nodded, her expression one of mild surprise. "If it has travelled here, it will travel beyond our borders, without doubt."

Agnes knew that this meant her parents would receive the news from the Grothi. She saw them as though they were in front of her, each sitting on a pew, waiting for the Grothi to deliver his sermon. He would stand before the crowd, fake benevolence rolling from him as if he were the tide itself. He would take pleasure in informing them of their son's death, and would remind them of their daughter's sins. Perhaps they thought she, too, was dead. Had her mother ever wished for life beyond the borders of

Locklear? Had her father dreamed of making swords for those in the capital city?

"I have to go back," Agnes said with a quiet breath, her voice a tremble.

"For what, Agnes?"

"I have to see...I have to see my parents. To see that they are well." As she said the words, Agnes knew that they were true. They did not know that another, better life, beyond the one they lived, existed. "And Godwin. To know that he is safe. A new life cannot wait within the seasons until the old life has been given away." The thought of seeing Godwin again made her throat sting, her blood pulse, her arms ache.

"So you will take my cloak," Bess said, swivelling towards her bedroom. "And you shall keep the hood up."

Agnes agreed, and swiftly, Nyx and Fly helped, showing Agnes a couple of pockets that Bess had sewn inside, and how the drawstring gathered around the neck. Within her pockets, they placed an apple and a water skin for her journey.

"It will take you two nights, and you must become one with the trees in the forest, Agnes. If soldiers have moved from beyond the kingdom to celebrate..." Bess let her words dance into the air unfinished, the girls watching their mother with shining eyes, not understanding the end of the sentence as the women did.

Agnes nodded, pulling up her cloak and looking out at the dusk of late spring as it quietly shifted into summer. The orange light had a melancholy glow, as though it knew that it could not protect Agnes from where she was to go, and what she might see.

"We wish you luck, and we shall see you soon."

The girls wrapped their small arms around Agnes' legs, whispering that they agreed they should see her soon. Agnes took a breath, and began the walk out of town, and towards the direction of Locklear, the place from which she had run with only a blanket upon her skin, no more than a month ago. It felt like a lifetime.

Chapter Forty-Four

The forest had transformed. Where once danger lurked, now a balmy air caressed Agnes' skin, the woodland's usual cacophony muted to a whisper. Phantom sounds flitted through the trees—laughter, hushed conversations, the soft fall of footsteps—only to vanish when she paused to listen.

Her hood remained up, and hours passed, the light's warmth fading. With every step, she drew nearer to a place that inspired both dread and an inexplicable yearning. Fear, she understood. But the longing? It coiled in the pit of her stomach, a hunger for familiar eyes—her mother's, her father's, and most achingly, Godwin's.

When the light changed again for the second time and began to filter through the trees, Agnes started to see things she recognised. The stream that she knew ran beyond her parents' house, to the tannery. Or, she reminded herself, what was the tannery. Now, it was a stream beside what was likely a pile of burned rubble. The leather, Silo's lovingly crafted chair—all consumed in their attempt to erase her. Yet here she stood, her continued existence a quiet defiance.

Soon, Agnes was on the periphery of the town. The sun was now in the sky, and she realised that her feet had led her full circle to the Widow Sewall's house. From the outside, it looked as it had before, as though the woman would be standing at the door, backlit by candles and a fire. But as Agnes rounded the building, illusion gave way to harsh reality—the door gaped open, an emptiness darker than night.

Agnes stepped into the house and looked about the room. There was nothing. Not a piece of furniture, not a tincture, not a stick of kindling. All was gone, absorbed into the town, into others' houses, fires.

It still had the scent of the Widow Sewall's home, however. The mould that grew at the base of the wooden slats that made up the wall, a smell not unlike a summer's day spent lying in the long grass beyond Agnes' childhood home. The scent of the stew that the Widow had simmering above the fire for days on end, added to when a scrap was procured from the market.

"Witch!"

Agnes' heartbeat began to pound loudly in her ears. Was it a real voice she heard, a true accusation?

"Witch!"

This time, another voice filtered through the muffled sound in her ears. She stepped to one side, hood still carefully covering her face, and hid behind the wall beside the open doorway, looking out.

There was no one there that she could see, no accusatory finger pointing in her direction. And yet, the voices grew.

"Witch!"

"Witch!"

Agnes leaned around further to look upon the path that led to the market, past Dunstable Farm. There were indeed people there, moving from their homes, crowding and surging forward. The voices became merged, no chants, no clear words any longer. Agnes checked her hood and stepped out of the house, unsure that to do this was the right thing. Without doubt, this was the Grothi's doing. This would be how he chose to deliver the news from the kingdom.

Agnes forced herself to walk terrified feet across the earth and down the path. She had no confidence to look at the farm, the huts, the houses that she knew so well. There was nothing that she would gain from a stolen glance at familiarity, but danger.

She quickly reached the back of the swarm, keeping her head down. Carefully, she listened to the talk of two women in front of her.

"She all but admitted it, sister."

"Is it true? I hear they kept her awake this past month. I'm sure she is delirious from lack of rest."

"And so she may be, and yet she names others."

"The Gods would let her rest if she be innocent."

Agnes felt her skin pulse. She knew of whom they spoke. That word that she had heard inside the Widow's empty house was not in her mind alone. She moved with the crowd along the streets that she had once called home. As the group of people swelled and filtered through, they came to the market square. But there was no market on today, no voices of joy in the soft mid-morning air. There, in front of Saskia's large stone house, was a structure.

Two thick and long sticks had been hammered into the ground, footholds decorating the sides. At the top, a shorter log sat, resting upon wooden cup shapes. Agnes viewed it with a growing unease, the skin on her hands damp and stinging. This was no ordinary day.

As if someone had spoken, the crowd suddenly fell silent, the people parting and creating a path to the rudimentary structure ahead. Agnes stepped back also, knowing who was about to walk the dirt between them. The Grothi appeared alone, dressed in his finest. He moved through the crowd without looking upon the faces, an expression of sublime calm tracking his features, a religious deity bound to walk the earth. When he reached the structure, he looked at it for longer than a moment. It was long enough for a gentle murmur to begin among the people, a curiosity. This was silenced when he held up his hand and turned to face them.

"And so we are here, and with thanks to Hildbrande, our master carpenter, for his work. Today, people of Locklear, we do something that we have not done in recent history. We condemn a witch with the kingdom's power behind us. Evil has been quickly spreading among the Principality of Hargothrest, and our gracious King and Queen have sent their instructions on how to deal with the demons walking among us."

Agnes felt a rage begin to burn in her stomach, moving up her body to her throat. The Grothi's words—a blatant lie that such accusations were rare—nearly provoked her to laughter. Did they not remember the women dragged into the woods? Her own ordeal by fire mere weeks ago?

"We now know that not all blessings are given by the Gods, interceded through myself. Some are taken, plucked from evil, without the knowledge of any of us here. We cannot be certain of our triumph over witchcraft until we eradicate those who have admitted to their crimes. And so, we have chosen to do this here, today, in such a way, to demonstrate to you, a warning. We are not afraid of you." The Grothi's eyes moved across the crowd, and Agnes ducked her head, heart pounding. He continued, "We will not come in the night to claim you for your crimes. We will not hide your punishment. You will pay as you should, before your peers, in the light of a blessed morning."

So, they had learned, Agnes thought. They no longer had to do away with witches in secret, for they were bolstered by an arrangement with an arrogant kingdom, fresh from success on the battlefield. The burning of her house had taught them the unpredictability of blessings. Rather than exposing the Grothi as a fraud, it had woven their beliefs tighter still. How many others had the Widow Sewall named? How many women in this very crowd harboured secret gifts, blessings not believed to be for the greater good?

Agnes let her eyes rise and looked beyond the Grothi to the structure. Movement above it caused her to glance up further, and there, at the top of Saskia's stone house, a window opened. In the window, the woman was sitting, looking out, her arms full. Godwin gazed down at the gallows with the joyful glee of a thriving child, and behind him, Saskia placed a kiss upon his head, eyes dancing.

Chapter Forty-Five

The Widow Sewall's arrival was heralded like a macabre festival. Agnes watched, throat tight, as the crowd bayed for blood. Storm clouds gathered, as if the Gods themselves had come to witness the demise of one of their blessed. The air was damp with the threat of rain, and Agnes raised her eyes to the sky, shadows forming above her. Perhaps the Gods were truly there, gathering.

"And so, Eira Sewall joins us now from her month of penance, during which she has confessed to her crimes of witchcraft," the Grothi said loudly, voice booming across the heads of the crowd.

Eira. A name Agnes had never before heard. Once a woman gained the respect of the title Widow, once she claimed her power, her land, and the strength within her, the first name was often never heard again. The Grothi had stripped the Widow Sewall of that respect.

The Grothi droned on, listing her crimes. "She is the enemy of all good. When questioned, Eira would not name her Gods. She spoke against us with wicked words."

Agnes looked upon the face of the Widow Sewall, who now stood behind the Grothi, eyes low. In truth, she was almost a different woman. Though her clothes had never been new, they had been cared for. Now they were threadbare, her shawl hanging from her small shoulders with barely a grip. An elderly woman, standing so small before them, was considered so great a threat.

The skies darkened above them, some groans from the crowd forming as the first few drops of rain fell. Agnes breathed in the earth and stone scents, looking up to the window once more to see Saskia holding Godwin's hand out to catch the drops, whispering in his ear. Had he ever been so engaged, so rosy-cheeked, with Agnes? The ache within her pulsed, sharp.

"The good and gracious Gods are pleased to save Locklear and our kingdom." The Grothi raised his voice louder to be heard above the noise of the quickening rain, the swell bouncing among stones and mud. "We condemn Eira Sewall to death."

He stepped aside, and it occurred to Agnes that this movement, and all, must have been practised. The Widow Sewall was promptly directed to stand beneath the structure. She did so, without any fight.

As the Widow was positioned beneath the gallows, Agnes recalled their agreement. She had promised to speak up, to repay the gift of a child. Yet Bess' words had sowed doubt. Was Godwin truly hers? Had the Widow known more than she let on? A rope was thrown with great accuracy over the top of the frame, and a man at the Widow's right-hand side caught it, then stood to attention. The Grothi nodded a singular, firm nod.

"Eira Sewall, have you any last words?" he asked, his voice booming through the square. The rain was now falling thick and fast, large drops soaking the people.

The Widow Sewall then seemed to remember a part of herself and looked up from the ground for the first time. Agnes breathed in sharply to see the bags beneath her eyes, dark and swollen, as though she had been punched. Her vision scanned the crowd, looking for a sympathetic face perhaps, and then, by chance or fate, she caught eyes with Agnes.

"No last words?" the Grothi prompted, and Agnes watched recognition dawn over the Widow Sewall's face. Her lips parted, and she whispered a word. Though Agnes could not hear her, she knew what she had said. She had whispered her name. Agnes felt her tongue begin to swell, the muscle heavy with words. She stared at the woman and silently begged the Gods to help her, hoping that she did not say her name again.

"What was that?" the Grothi asked, leaning in closer. "Speak again, woman, for your voice was not so quiet when you cursed this town."

Agnes stepped backwards swiftly, fearful, knocking into someone behind her.

"Oi! Mind yourself, stranger," came the response, and as a reflex, Agnes reached her hand up to make sure her hood still covered her hair. Despite this, the Widow had known her face.

"Be you friend in the crowd," the Widow suddenly said, voice lifting. A hush fell across the people, and they watched, stunned, listening ever closer. "Be you friend, speak. Speak my innocence."

Agnes reached her hand to her throat and tried to look away, to look anywhere but the Widow's eyes. She could not.

"There is no one to speak your innocence, witch," the Grothi interjected. "If there were, it should not matter. You have already confessed your sins before the Gods."

At this, the Widow Sewall dropped her gaze to the ground. Agnes saw the defeat, saw the realisation that it would be worthless at this late stage. Should she speak up, raise her voice, she would only find death. Two witches, hanging beside each other, feet blowing in the wind, were surely not better than one.

The Grothi murmured something to his helper, who swiftly placed the noose over the Widow Sewall's neck and stood back to attention. The crowd began to grow restless then, as though they had been waiting for years, for centuries, to find this woman guilty. As if the world had been waiting for a hanging, and but two more moments would be agonising for all but the Gods. Murmurings and noise began to filter above the heads, jeering and booing alike.

"Draw her up," the Grothi said, turning to the crowd. Agnes forced herself to watch, to see the Widow Sewall's final moments. As the rope was pulled taught, the man began to climb the footholds on the side of the structure, keeping the rope tight in his hand. When finally at the top, he used those same footholds to create a winch, and slowly, though it seemed the cruellest way to do it, the Widow was raised into the air.

Agnes watched her eyes, hoping that they might make contact again, that she would comfort her with her gaze. Instead, the Widow looked up to the sky, where the rain fell, and into the clouds. As though she knew not where she was and felt not what was happening to her body, her eyes brightened. Her skin flushed with colour, pink cheeks, the deep rivets on her skin smoothing. She let out a laugh, a single noise that stunned the crowd into silence. There, in the rain, the Widow laughed again.

"Ah, there you are!" she said, and the crowd looked skyward, including Agnes, to see where her eyes fell. The clouds had parted just a little, the sun burning bright beyond them, casting a glow upon the Widow. Agnes smiled. She knew that she could not see what the Widow Sewall could see, but such mirth only came from one place. Love. She turned back to face the scene and saw that it was done. The Widow's feet now hung above the ground, lifeless. Her face, despite all that had just passed across it, was her own again, and yet, it was different. It was free from pain.

"Aren't you——?" Agnes heard the words at her left side, hands reaching up to her hood. It had fallen.

Chapter Forty-Six

To flee would have drawn more attention, so Agnes simply pulled her hood up and turned away, pushing herself through the dispersing crowd of villagers. Who had spoken, she wasn't sure, but it was the voice of a woman, and it was not her mother.

Her mother. Where were her parents? As she moved through the crowd, she listened to the people, trying to hear their voices.

"Sad in a way, she helped deliver my child..."

"Well, and my neighbour's. But you never know, do you? You never can tell which—"

"There was that other one, wasn't there? The blacksmith's daughter. Said they hung her in the woods, mind you, I've seen no proof."

"Saskia at the stone house, I heard she's been teaching the women to carve protection into their front doors. Anywhere the woman could come in again, that's the trick."

Agnes breathed in the dank, wet air, smelling the bodies around her as the dampness on their clothes mingled with their sour sweat. She forged through, one goal in mind. She would reach the blacksmith's house and then leave via the woods, following the stream, until she was safely in her new life, knowing her parents were well. She had seen Godwin, seen his thriving being. She could offer nothing that he didn't now have. She was no longer Mother.

She continued, feeling the townsfolk milling away to their homes, the task of the day now done. It was as though nothing had happened. Voices filled the air, laughter, joy. At one point, Agnes heard a song drifting through the street and turned to see a woman bringing in her washing from the rain, her voice lifting. How could life carry on as though nothing had changed, when they had just watched a woman put to death? Agnes breathed in the dank air and turned her face to the blacksmiths a little out of town. It was because life would continue, inevitably. It would continue long after her feet left the muddied ground, too.

Eventually, she found herself walking alone to the house. Had her parents been among those baying for the Widow's blood? For what would they do with such a moment except imagine their own daughter there? Perhaps they hid, already aware of her brother's fate. Or maybe she could spare them that knowledge, warn them away from future spectacles.

As she neared, she heard voices. The forge was lit, the air around it wobbling as though in a dream. Agnes saw the tools laid out, ready for work.

"Will you have soup?" her mother's voice said softly, to which her father grunted. Agnes took a breath. She had meant to see them, to check that they were well, but now she stood in front of their door, and knew that she would not leave without making herself known.

She raised a hand to knock and let it fall upon the wood a single time. It opened almost immediately, and there stood her father, eyes wide.

"Agnes."

"What?" her mother said, pulling her father aside. Both stood staring at her as though she were an apparition.

"You cannot be here," her mother said, gaze hardening. "They have just hung Sewall—"

Agnes raised a hand to silence them. "The Widow Sewall. Yes, I am aware. I have come to deliver news to you of your son before you hear it in church."

Her father and mother glanced at each other, and her father raised his hand to his forehead, sweat visible on his brow.

"Agnes, if they catch you here—" he began.

"They shall hang me," she finished, voice flat.

"No. That is not what your father was going to say," her mother interrupted, leaning her hand on the door, as though she were about to slam it. "If they catch you here, they will punish us. We fear the Gods, unlike you, and the Grothi is ever clear on what he expects from his townsfolk. Tell us what news of your brother, and allow us to go back to our life. For what we did to deserve such children must have been wicked indeed."

Agnes' jaw slackened, shocked by her mother's venom. Her father studied the ground, avoiding her gaze. They were worse than before, their anger calcified in her absence.

She bowed her head, delivering the news with a whisper, for though they deserved little contrition, they were still her parents.

"The kingdom has defeated the rebels. They have won the war. All who opposed have been slaughtered," she whispered.

"And so, the Gods will it," her father responded, before the door was shut in her face. Agnes inspected it for a moment, unable to take her gaze from the image she had not noticed when she had arrived. Upon the door was a mark that was brand new. Two Vs overlapped each other, delved deep into the wood, forming a strange W.

Agnes turned and walked to the furnace, a new goal forming in her mind. She would not go along the stream and into the woods just yet. With a hand, she reached into the flame and selected one of the hot coals from among its friends. Swiftly, she turned, ensuring her hood was still up, and stepped with a light foot back down into town.

The people had largely gone about their business now, and as Agnes walked through the streets and to the square, she saw that though the frame remained, the Widow Sewall's body was now gone. A few children played around it, pretending to be the Widow and the man who took her life, laughing and sticking their tongues out of the sides of their mouths, the whole thing a game. Agnes watched for a moment and then glanced up at the window beyond. It was now shut, the owners of the house somewhere inside, Godwin no doubt laughing, his memories of Agnes forgotten. Her hand closed around the coal.

She moved on towards the end of the square, where the church stood. Who would be in there? Perhaps no one at this time of day. On the other hand, the Grothi could be in there, working one-on-one with a village member or the Widow Pluck. Agnes' eyes raised to the thatched roof, fell to the interlocking system of timber frames and smiled.

"May the Gods forgive you," she whispered, hurling the coal onto the thatch. Despite the earlier rain, the wind fanned the ember to life. A tendril of flame licked upward, hungry and insistent. The embers shared their fiery secrets quickly, kissing the straw with fondness. Agnes turned away, striding towards the forest. She knew that by the time the trees enveloped her, black smoke would be billowing above Locklear as it had once before.

Without the church, the people would flock to the fields, stand with their feet in the mud, and watch the Grothi as he tried to make an excuse for their chilled skin. Agnes thought with strange satisfaction of the words that might fall from his lips, his desperate gaze as he viewed the remnants of his church. Her thoughts moved to the tanner's house, of the flame that licked her skin and how readily he must have lit that fire, encouraging others to do the same. It was as he always said, after all: a life for a death.

Phlegm for phlegm.

Flame for flame.

Fire.

ACKNOWLEDGEMENTS AND NOTES

Thank you, reader, for taking the time to step inside Locklear with Agnes. The history of using the word 'witch' as an accusation is complicated, and what is most complex of all is that this is still an issue in parts of the world today. Witch trials and persecution against those called witches are still taking place. What makes a woman a witch? Is it speaking out against those in power, behaving in a way believed to be outside of the norm, or using natural ingredients to attempt to heal an illness?

Whether you believe the Widow Sewall to be a witch or not is up to you. Whether Godwin is Agnes' child or Saskia's is up to you. Opinion and belief form an accusation of witchcraft and persecution. Proof is a very different thing.

A huge thank you to:

My mother, Hilary, who supports all of my stories, long and short, in her genre or not. Your thoughts are so valuable to me.

My husband, Daniel, who listens, supports endlessly, brings tea, and has really gone above and beyond in the quest for accurate medieval research. Thank you for coming to banquets with me, trying the turnip soups I make, dressing up for medieval events, and showing such genuine interest.

To Charley, my writing coach, who listened for hours as I waxed lyrical about whether or not chimneys should be included in Agnes' world, and always takes the time to discuss ideas with me. You make me a better writer.

Thank you to the rest of my family (Marilyn, Peter, Dad, Evan, Clare, Anna, and Adam), who may not have been directly involved in the writing of Witchborne but who supported me in other ways.

Of course, no acknowledgement is complete without a sincere thank you to Scronge, my dog, who is an expert at knowing when it is time to take a break. I'm sorry there are no large dogs in this story. Maybe the next one.

ABOUT THE AUTHOR

Rachel Grosvenor is a writer from Birmingham, now based in Wales, with a PhD, MA and BA in Creative Writing. She is the author of 'The Finery' (spotlighted in The Guardian), 'The Birth of Ida', and 'Witchborne'. When not writing, she is a writing coach and editor for dedicated authors. She spends the rest of her time walking her large poodle Scronge and wondering what's for elevenses.

Book Club Questions

1. What does the medieval and fantastical world of Locklear offer that a contemporary, urban setting, for example, does not? How did this help to execute the aims of the novel?
2. How do Agnes's feelings of insignificance and inadequacy shape her journey? How does she battle through them?
3. In what ways does Agnes's gift threaten the traditional gender roles that are in place?
4. What were your first impressions of Pa? Did your opinions about him change throughout the novel?
5. Scent is used extensively to describe different characters and their backgrounds. Why is this done? What does this represent?
6. How do the religious traditions in Locklear shape the community's future? What role does the Grothi play in the society's ability to evolve?
7. Do you think Saskia ever actually cared about the wellbeing of Agnes? To what extent is Anges and Saskia's rivalry facilitated by the patriarchy?
8. Do you see Godwin as Agnes's son, or Saskia's? What does this confusion say about bodily autonomy and human rights in the novel?
9. What does the kingdom represent, and why are the people of Bess's village so against it? Why are women's lives in Locklear so linear, when in Bess's village, the women seem to have complete freedom?
10. Agnes is characterised by the lies she tells people, so, why does she decide to be upfront and truthful to Bess?

11. What do you think Silo and his father's future will look like, following the events of the novel? Do you think they will be held to the same standards as Agnes's parents?
12. Do you think Anges's revenge on the Grothi resulted in any real change for the people of Locklear?

About Fly on the Wall Press

A publisher with a conscience.
Political, Sustainable, Ethical.
Publishing politically-engaged, international fiction, poetry and cross-genre anthologies on pressing issues. Founded in 2018 by founding editor, Isabelle Kenyon.

Some other publications:

The Soul We Share by Ricky Ray

The Unpicking by Donna Moore

Lying Perfectly Still by Laura Fish

Modern Gothic - Anthology

And I Will Make of You a Vowel Sound by Morag Anderson

The Dark Within Them by Isabelle Kenyon

The Wager and the Bear by John Ironmonger

The Process of Poetry Edited by Rosanna McGlone

The Others by Sheena Kalayil

Demos Rising Edited by Isabelle Kenyon

These Mothers of Gods by Rachel Bower

The Truth Has Arms and Legs by Alice Fowler

The Devil's Draper by Donna Moore

The State of Us by Charlie Hill

The Sleepless by Liam Bell

Social Media:

@fly_press (X)

@flyonthewallpress (Instagram, Bluesky, Facebook, Tiktok)

www.flyonthewallpress.co.uk